TRAIL OF
THE SKULLS

TRAIL OF
THE SKULLS

WAYNE C. LEE

Thorndike Press • Chivers Press
Thorndike, Maine USA   Bath, England

This Large Print edition is published by Thorndike Press, USA
and by Chivers Press, England.

Published in 1997 in the U.S. by arrangement with Golden
West Literary Agency.

Published in 1998 in the U.K. by arrangement with Golden
West Literary Agency.

U.S. Hardcover   0-7862-1197-0   (Western Series Edition)
U.K. Hardcover   0-7540-3075-X   (Chivers Large Print)

The text of this Large Print edition is unabridged.
Other aspects of the book may vary from the original edition.

Set in 16 pt. Plantin by Warren S. Doersam.

Printed in the United States on permanent paper.

British Library Cataloguing in Publication Data available

Library of Congress Cataloging in Publication Data

Lee, Wayne C.
    Trail of the skulls / by Wayne C. Lee.
        p.   cm.
    ISBN 0-7862-1197-0 (lg. print : hc : alk. paper)
    1. Large type books. I. Title.
    [PS3523.E34457T7   1997]
    813'.54—dc21   97-36732

TRAIL OF
THE SKULLS

CHAPTER 1

Jason Trent rode into Trail City that April afternoon in 1886 from the flat plains to the north. He had been in the saddle several days since leaving the sandhills of Nebraska, and even the hastily slapped-together buildings of Trail City looked inviting.

But Trail City offered more than just a place of rest and refreshment. Here he hoped to find the means for making the money he needed to make a good start on his little Nebraska ranch.

As he rode slowly down Trail Street, which cut the town in half, he sensed the feeling of urgency that permeated the town. The buildings had been hastily erected. Some were not yet finished, and carpenters were busy in several places.

A year ago this had been open prairie without a sign of civilization except for the Santa Fe railroad tracks that cut a steel path toward the mountains a hundred and fifty miles to the west. A mile south of the tracks, the Arkansas River slowed to a gentle pace and

7

meandered off to the east toward Dodge City.

One building along the street stood out in sharp contrast to its neighbors. That was the Culver Hotel. Built of limestone blocks, standing strong and defiant, it dominated everything up and down Trail Street. Trent rode past the hotel toward a sign on a big barn at the south end of the street, "Trail's End." There were corrals behind the barn, and a windmill stood by a big tank, its wheel turning methodically in the breeze.

As Trent moved down the street, he again felt the urgency that gripped the town. It seemed to whisper that any man who hesitated would miss out on the bonanza this new town was offering.

He passed Sparrow's Saloon, the only place that was busy at the moment. To the north and across on the west side of the street, he had noticed the Longhorn Saloon. It had some business but nothing compared to Sparrow's.

Trent reined in at the barn, noticing again the big sign, "Trail's End. I. P. Olive, prop." A man stepped out to take Trent's horse.

"Staying in Trail long?" the man asked.

"Just till tomorrow," Trent said. "Any cattle-buyers in town?"

"Not yet. But there will be. This place will

be busting at the seams this summer. Plenty of buyers then."

"Give my horse a good feed," Trent said. "He's been over a lot of country."

The man grinned, his teeth flashing. "Most of them have been when they come to Trail."

Trent looked to the south, where a dozen men were frantically building pens and loading chutes beside a new rail siding. "Looks like this place is expecting plenty of business," he said.

"It sure is," the man said. "Don't worry about your horse, Mister. Old Sam will take care of him."

Trent turned back up the street, noticing Bob Wright's trail-outfitting store and Martin Culver's saddlery and harness store. Beyond the hotel was a real-estate office and H. M. Beverly's general merchandise store. Whoever had told Trent that half the businessmen of Dodge City were putting up stores out here at Trail City had been partly right, at least.

Trent went into the hotel, wondering if there was any point in his stopping here tonight; he could have camped out on the trail south of the Arkansas. The sooner he got down to the panhandle and got his cattle and came back, the better chance he had of hit-

9

ting a good market. But he wanted a soft bed and a hot meal.

At the desk, Trent asked for a room and inquired again about buyers for the summer. He was assured there would be buyers swarming over the place by June.

As he started up the stairs, he met two men coming down. Trent wouldn't have given them a second glance if the smaller of the men hadn't bumped him in passing.

The man apologized in a soft voice, then Trent saw him give a slight nod to his companion, a big man that Trent guessed must weigh two hundred and thirty or forty pounds and stand six feet three or four inches tall. Something about the look the little man gave the big one touched a spark of suspicion in Trent.

He went on up to his room, pushing the incident from his mind. He was just jumpy because of the money he was carrying, the money that represented so much of his life.

The money belt he wore held three thousand dollars, borrowed from Herb Hartline, the man Trent had worked for up in the sandhills before he took out papers on a little parcel of land and started his own ranch. Trent hoped to parlay that money into a lot more. But if anything happened to it, it would leave him with a debt he couldn't pay even by forfeiting his ranch.

Before preparing for supper in the hotel dining room, he relaxed on the bed for half an hour. Then he left his room and went down to the hotel veranda just as the sun was dropping out of sight beyond Cheyenne Creek, which angled into the Arkansas a short distance west of town. He was still there when the supper bell sounded.

He went back inside and found a place at the long table in the dining room. He had just sat down when the two men he had bumped into on the stairway sat down beside him.

"My name is Cole Spark," the big fellow said amiably, "and this is Vane Fanok."

Trent nodded. "I'm Jason Trent. I ranch up in Nebraska."

"Long way from home, ain't you?" Fanok asked. "This should be a busy time of year for you."

"Busy enough," Trent said. "I'm going after a herd down in Texas."

"We're from Texas," Spark said. "Up here looking over the situation. We plan to ship out about twenty-five hundred head from Trail City this summer."

"Looks like they'll be ready for you," Trent said.

"Reckon so," Spark said. "But we had to be sure. We heard all kinds of rumors about this town. It's going to be a button-buster this summer — as wild as Dodge used to be before they clamped on that quarantine."

"We're plenty close to Kansas now," Fanok said. "You can step to the back door and spit across the line."

"Where are you getting your cattle?" Spark asked.

"Got a cousin in the panhandle, Bill Ellis," Trent said. "He's got some cattle to sell, and I figure his price will be cheap."

Spark nodded at Fanok. "You can buy critters for about ten dollars a head there. They'll be worth twenty-five or thirty here at the railroad. Good money if you're man enough to get them here."

They ate in silence. These were the only two men in town who had shown him friendliness, but somehow he couldn't respond to their show of friendship. Maybe he was edgy, or maybe it was instinct, like that of an animal guarding the location of his secret den.

Supper over, the two men stood up. "Long evening ahead of us," Spark said. "What shall we do?"

"How about a game over at Sparrow's?" Fanok asked casually.

Trent looked at the little man, so sharp a

contrast to his companion. Fanok was about five and a half feet tall and weighed nearly a hundred pounds less than Cole Spark. Trent tabbed him as a professional gambler. He had no business playing cards with him, not even in a friendly game.

"I think I'll turn in pretty soon," he said. "I'm not much of a gambler."

Trent went outside with the men and watched them walk down the street and disappear into Sparrow's saloon. Darkness had settled over the town. About the only lights visible came from the hotel and the two saloons, Sparrow's and the Longhorn. Not many other businesses were open yet, and the men who were working so frantically to get the town ready for the big rush this summer were either in one of the lighted buildings or had gone to bed.

It was still a little early for bed, Trent thought, so he angled across the street toward the Longhorn Saloon. He noticed I. P. Olive's name on the sign. Evidently the Longhorn was owned by the same man who owned the Trail's End Stable. He'd heard of "Print" Olive. Everybody in the Nebraska sandhills had heard of him. Trent knew that Print Olive had left his ranch on the Dismal and Loup rivers in Nebraska and gone to Dodge City. But he hadn't expected to find him here.

After a few minutes at the Longhorn, Trent turned back toward the hotel. Tomorrow he hoped to get an early start. He had learned all he needed to of this town.

He crossed the street and turned toward the hotel. At the corner, a hand suddenly grabbed his arm and jerked him back into the shadows at the side of the building.

Trent started to yell, but his breath was driven from him by a huge fist slammed into his stomach. Trent wheeled around, getting his back to the wall of the hotel, and lashed out at the men who had jumped him. It was too dark to see faces, but he was sure there were two, maybe three.

He landed a couple of blows that brought painful grunts, then a fist caught him on the side of the head and he ducked away from it only to be slammed by another fist on the other side. He wheeled toward this assailant and got the satisfaction of connecting with a solid fist.

But then the man behind him caught one arm and before Trent could swing around, he had the other arm, too. The man was powerful. Although Trent struggled furiously, he couldn't break the grip as both his arms were jerked up behind his back. Then the smaller man moved up close and slammed his fists into Trent's face and stomach.

Consciousness slipped away, but through the haze he thought he recognized the little man in front of him. Vane Fanok. If Fanok was slugging him, then it must be Cole Spark holding him.

Trent fought to keep his head, trying to find a way to break free. But there was no way. He slumped forward and the blows stopped. The big man let go of his arms, and Trent slid to the ground against the wall of the hotel.

He wanted to get up, but there wasn't enough strength in his body even to lift his head. So he lay there, every part of him beaten into submission except his brain.

"Looks like he's out cold," the big man said.

"Should be," the little man replied. "I almost broke a fist slugging him."

"Where's that money belt you said you felt?"

The little man flipped open Trent's shirt and jerked on the belt's buckle.

"Hurry it up," another voice said in a whisper.

Vaguely, Trent recognized the new voice as that of a woman. But he couldn't turn his head to look even if there had been enough light. Even in his semiconscious state, he realized that it had to be Cole Spark and Vance Fanok who had attacked him. Nobody else in Trail City could have known he was wearing a money belt. Fanok must have felt it when he bumped into him on the stairway.

Then the money belt came loose and was slipped out from under Trent's shirt. A moment later, he was alone in the dark. His mind became even fuzzier.

It was still dark when he regained consciousness. He stirred, finding that he could move. He got to his feet and staggered to the front of the hotel. There was a dim light in the lobby, but there were no light now either in the Longhorn or Sparrow's Saloon.

Trent felt sick. He thought of going after Spark and Fanok. But he knew if he found them, he didn't have strength enough to do a thing about recovering his money. He would have to wait till morning.

He staggered into the empty lobby and up the stairs to his room, and threw himself across the bed without pulling off his boots. He sank into a restless sleep in which he dreamed he was fighting robbers. When he finally woke, daylight was creeping into the room.

He got up and poured some water into the

basin in the corner of the room and soused his face. He felt better. But he'd never feel good again, he thought, unless he recovered that money. Without it, he'd lose his ranch to Herb Hartline, not to mention his dream of getting a start in the cattle business.

He went downstairs to eat, and looked around as others came down to breakfast, but neither Spark nor Fanok appeared. When breakfast was over, he went to the desk and asked about them.

"They're gone," the clerk said. "I didn't see them check out, but they left more than enough to pay for their lodging so it's no skin off my nose when they left or where they went."

Trent went outside, impatience prodding him. Somehow he hadn't expected thieves as brazen as Spark and Fanok to tuck their tails and run. But they were gone and he had to find them.

At the barn, Trent found Sam. "Did two fellows, a big one and a little one, pull out during the night?" he asked.

"I reckon they did," Sam said. "Along about midnight, or before, I heard a commotion out here and came to see. They were just leaving."

"Which way did they go?"

Sam pointed to the south. "Headed for

Texas, I reckon. Cole Spark's old man owns a big spread down there."

Trent thanked the man, paid his bill from some change in his pocket, and got on his horse. It would be a hard ride catching up with Spark and Fanok. They had a six-hour start on him. But it was a long way to Texas, and if they stayed on the trail, he'd catch them somewhere between Trail City and Texas.

This time, Trent wouldn't be caught without his gun in his hand.

CHAPTER 2

It was a warm day, but Trent drove his horse relentlessly. The trail was easy to follow, although it was still only dimly stamped into the prairie. Just a few cattle had come up this trail last fall after Martin Culver had marked it out. There would be many more this summer.

At times, Trent saw the bleached buffalo skulls that Culver had used to mark the trail. Back in Ogallala, Trent had heard this trail that Culver had so hastily marked called the trail of the skulls. Culver had used buffalo skulls wherever he could find enough of them. In other places he had used pyramids of buffalo chips. If this was like most trails up from Texas, there would soon be skulls bleaching here that had never belonged to buffaloes.

Trent halted at a small stream, watered and fed his horse, then ate his supper. He wished he could keep moving, but he needed daylight to follow the trail.

As he settled into his blankets, he found some consolation in the fact that the trail

Spark and Fanok were taking led in the direction Trent had planned to ride, anyway. Both were going toward Texas.

Sunup found Trent in the saddle again, his hope of catching Spark and Fanok brightening with the dawn. The months ahead, which had looked so rosy when he left his sandhills ranch, would be as bleak as a cold December day if he didn't recover his money.

He thought of the letter he had received from his cousin, Bill Ellis, and the big dreams it had set off. Ellis had written that he and three neighbors in the Texas panhandle were being squeezed out by big ranchers, and if they didn't do something in a hurry, they would lose everything they had. Last year, Ellis had said, the big ranchers had demanded that the little fellows get out, but now they were also demanding that they leave their cattle. They said the cattle belonged to them because those cattle had fattened on grass the big fellows claimed.

Trent had thought he had seen a way to help his cousin and himself at the same time. He had persuaded Herb Hartline that the idea was sound, although Trent had to mortgage his little ranch to Herb to get the loan.

With three thousand dollars, Trent was sure he could buy at least three hundred head of cattle from his cousin and his neighbors. He'd trail those cattle north, sell part of the herd at Trail City — enough to pay off his loan to Herb — then take the rest of the cattle on to his ranch. He'd have all the cattle his ranch could handle. Instead of struggling for years to build up a herd, he'd have his herd in one summer.

Herb Hartline had been hard to convince. He couldn't understand how Trent expected to get those cattle out of the country if Bill Ellis couldn't get them out himself. But Trent was sure he had the answer. The big ranchers wouldn't fight a cattle-buyer who came in and legally bought the cattle. They had no quarrel with anyone except the little ranchers they wanted to swallow up.

That was how Trent had reasoned when he left Nebraska. A few doubts had filtered into his mind by the time he got to Trail City, but those had been forgotten when he had lost his money.

Toward evening of the third day, Trent came within hailing distance of a rider, and he spurred his weary horse into a gallop to catch him. The rider spotted him and stopped, but when Trent reined up, he saw that the man had his gun out of the holster,

21

resting on his leg.

"Am I still in Colorado?" Trent asked, ignoring the gun.

"You're in Texas now. Quite a ways from Colorado. You must have crossed the line from the Territory sometime this afternoon."

Trent nodded. "Ever hear of a man named Spark down here?"

The man squinted his eyes as he studied Trent. "Sure. Old Ira Spark and his boy, Cole, own the S Bar spread down that way." He pointed to the southeast.

"Far?" Trent asked.

"Day-and-a-half or two-day ride, I reckon," the man said.

Trent thanked the man and nudged his horse on. The man had pointed in the general direction of Bill Ellis' ranch. After Trent found Spark and Fanok and settled with them, he'd see Ellis.

On the fifth day out of Trail City, Trent began to see more and more ranches. He estimated it would take something like twenty days to drive a herd over the ground he had ridden in five. His horse was all in, and he was little better.

Seeing a ranch headquarters off to the side of his course, he reined that way. It was best, he decided, to find out where the S Bar was so he wouldn't pass it or ride into it unexpectedly.

The place was run down; the buildings looked old from lack of paint or repair. They were big enough to be the headquarters of a large ranch, but Trent guessed they probably belonged to a small rancher who had had grand ideas.

There was no stir around the place when he rode up and stopped at the hitchrack. A few horses were drowsing in the corral, but a dog that had been lying in the shade of the house suddenly charged out, barking furiously.

Still, nobody came from the house, and Trent could see no sign of life other than the dog and the horses. He thought he heard a door slam, but nobody appeared.

Then a man stepped around the corner of the house. Trent turned to look and felt his blood run cold. It was partly from the sight of the gun in the man's hand, but it was more the man himself. Trent would never forget Cole Spark's moonlike face.

"So you trailed us, did you?" Spark said, and Trent heard both anger and indecision in his voice.

"I've been looking for you," Trent said, recovering from his surprise. "You borrowed something of mine, and I want it back."

"I don't borrow things," Spark said. "But it looks like you borrowed plenty of trouble."

Another man came out the front door then, and Trent turned his head to see Vane Fanok.

"What do we do with him, Cole?" Fanok asked.

"Reckon there's only one thing we can do," Spark said matter-of-factly.

"I hadn't planned on anything like this," Fanok said.

"A man handles things the way they come, not the way he plans," Spark said. "Get down off your horse, Trent."

Trent swung down stiffly, and Cole Spark watched every move he made. He had no illusions about what Spark planned to do. When he was on the ground, he turned to face Spark. But just then the door opened again and another man, as big as Cole but with graying hair and a slower gait, appeared on the sagging porch.

"What have you got there, Cole?" he demanded in a deep voice.

"Fellow named Trent, Pa," Cole said.

"The cattle-buyer you met up in Trail City?"

"That's him," Fanok put in. "Looks like he don't learn lessons very well."

"We'll soon teach him," Cole said. "And this time he won't forget."

The older man's heavy eyebrows pulled down in a frown. "Hold on, Cole. There are some things we don't want happening on the S Bar."

"Nobody will ever know he came here," Cole said.

"How do you know that?" Ira Spark demanded.

Cole twisted uncomfortably. "He just rode in from Colorado. How could anyone know?"

"It's fool reasoning like that that gets a man hanged," Ira said irritably.

"Want us to put him in the guest room and treat him like a king?" Cole snapped.

"Pull his fangs and boot him out," Ira said. "With no money or guns, he should be glad to sneak back where he came from."

Cole scowled at Trent. "Toss over your gun," he demanded. "Careful with it — Vane, get his rifle."

Trent slowly lifted his gun out of its holster and let it drop. Cole inched forward and kicked the gun to one side. Trent saw Vane Fanok move over to his horse and take the rifle out of its boot.

Ira Spark stepped down into the yard. "Now that you've lost your stingers, Mr.

Trent, get on your horse and ride out of this country — and don't come back!"

Trent, rage boiling inside him, turned and mounted. There was nothing else he could do in the face of Cole Spark's gun. Only Ira Spark's caution about killing a man on the S Bar had saved his life, and he knew it.

Trent reined his horse around and made him walk out of the yard. He fought the urge to spur his horse into a dead run. The hair on the back of his neck crawled as he could almost feel a bullet slamming into his back.

Once away from the S Bar, he turned and looked back. The three men were still standing where he had left them. Trent turned back and nudged his horse into a trot, heading back to the northwest.

But once over the first knoll, out of sight of the buildings, he reined up. He didn't know just where he would go but one thing was sure: he wasn't tucking his tail and running, the way Ira Spark seemed to think he would. He hadn't ridden over two hundred miles from Trail City to find the men who had robbed him only to turn tail and run the moment he did find them.

He reined his horse to the left, keeping the knoll between him and the S Bar buildings. He must be within fifty miles of Bill's place, although he didn't know just where it was. He had been riding in the right direction ever since he left Trail City. His cousin's ranch was probably the only place in Texas where he could get a gun without stealing it.

Well out of sight of the S Bar, Trent reined to the southeast again, looking for another ranch. He found one before he had gone far. It was small, and Trent rode in bravely. He reached the hitchrack in front of the small clapboard house and was just swinging down when a sharp voice halted him.

"Hold it right there, Mister!"

He jerked up his head, one foot on the ground, the other still in the stirrup. A girl was standing on the tiny porch, pointing a rifle at him. She was small and had the blackest hair Trent had ever seen. But he concentrated on the rifle.

"What have I done?" he demanded.

"Who are you? What do you want?"

"I'm looking for information," Trent said, still not moving.

"Get your foot down," the girl snapped. "You look like a goose in a rainstorm."

Trent stepped to the ground and faced the girl.

"I don't have a gun," he said.

"I saw a man shot once by a gambler who said he didn't have a gun," she retorted.

"Now, who are you? What information do you want?"

"Name's Jason Trent. I'm looking for a man named Bill Ellis. Is his ranch anywhere near here?"

"Did you come from the S Bar?"

Trent nodded slowly, seeing the girl's grip on the rifle tighten. "That's where I lost my hardware. Seems they didn't like the idea of me riding over the country with guns."

"You're not working for Spark?"

"Hardly," Trent said bitterly. "I was looking for Cole Spark to settle a score with him. When I found him, he had the drop on me."

The muzzle of the rifle lowered slowly. "We've got a score to settle with Ira and Cole Spark, too. Why are you looking for Bill Ellis?"

"He's my cousin," Trent said.

A rider charged into the yard and pulled his horse back on its haunches. "Who's this jasper, Beth?" he demanded.

"Says his name is Trent," the girl said. "He's looking for Bill Ellis."

The men looked at each other sharply. The man was under six feet tall, of medium build, with dark hair and eyes, matching the girl's.

"I heard Bill say he was expecting you," the man said finally. "I'm Andy Gilman. You ran into my sister, Beth. The Gilmans own

28

this spread, no matter what Ira Spark says."

"Does my cousin live close?" Trent asked eagerly.

"About two crow-hops to the south," Andy said. "I can take you there."

"Don't trust him too far," Beth Gilman warned. "He admits he came from the S Bar."

Andy turned a frown on Trent. "What were you doing there?"

"Losing my Colt and my rifle," Trent said. He shot a glance at the girl. Beth Gilman was still not convinced of his peaceful intentions. Judging from the way she gripped the rifle, she was not one to be crossed carelessly.

"Let's go," Andy said, and Trent mounted and reined his horse around.

It was a short ride to Bill Ellis's ranch, as Andy had said, but the sun was nearly down when they rode in. Ellis was just walking from his barn toward the house. He recognized Trent, and ran forward.

"Jason! I'm glad to see you!" he exclaimed.

"Are things any better than they were?" Trent asked, dismounting.

Ellis shook his head. "Worse, I'm afraid."

CHAPTER 3

Trent thanked Andy Gilman for directing him to his cousin's ranch, then turned with Bill Ellis and went into the house. Ellis introduced Trent to his wife, a tall brunette.

"Now then," Trent said, "let's hear the worst."

"It's about like it was when I wrote," Ellis said. "Only now the big fellows are giving us just so much time to pack up and get out. They won't let us take a thing with us except some household goods and the shirts on our backs."

"Where do they get the legal right for that?" Trent demanded.

"In their gun belts," Ellis said. He held up a hand as Trent started to object. "I know. You'll say we're living in a civilized age. Just try telling that to Ira Spark."

"How many of these big ranchers are pushing you?"

"Spark is the main one — he's the biggest. He's the closest to us, and he's the meanest. We could handle the others all right, but not

30

Ira Spark. He plans to take over this entire valley."

Trent scowled. "The only way to talk to some people is with lead." He tapped his empty holster. "The Sparks relieved me even of that privilege."

"You've tangled with the Sparks?"

Trent nodded. "Twice. The first time was in Trail City. Cole Spark and his little buddy, Vane Fanok, jumped me in an alley, beat me up and took my money belt. I was figuring on buying your cattle and trailing them north. I thought the big ranchers might let a cattle-buyer through."

"They wouldn't," Ellis said. "I guess you got that answer when they stole your money in Trail City."

Trent nodded. "At the time, I figured they were just after the money. Now I've got a hunch there was more to it than that."

"I reckon," Ellis said. "Did you tell them where you were going?"

"Not exactly," Trent said, trying to remember what he had said. "But I think I might have let your name slip. Never figured anybody way up there would have heard of you."

"I thought you were more careful than that, Jason," Ellis said. "I suppose you trailed Spark down here to get your money. But you won't get it back from Cole Spark unless you kill him — which might not be a bad idea. How much did you lose?"

"Three thousand dollars. I figured on buying about three hundred head of cattle here, and I thought I could sell them at Trail City for twenty-five dollars a head. I gathered from your letter that you didn't plan on trying to get out with your herd."

"I don't see how I can."

"Would you be willing to try if I ramrodded the drive?"

Ellis paced the floor. "I'd rather sell right here for ten dollars than take my chances on twenty-five at Trail City. I don't figure I can get to Trail, even with you heading up the drive."

"I can't buy your herd," Trent said. "So the only chance I've got of raising three thousand dollars to pay off Herb Hartline is to help you get your stuff to market for a share of your profit and then hope you'll stake me to the rest of the money I'll need to pay off my debt."

Ellis sighed. "Sounds good, but it will take more than words to get past Spark's outfit."

"How many other outfits can you get to go in with you?"

"I've got three neighbors the S Bar is planning to swallow up this summer," Ellis said.

"The Gilmans, Dade Tovar, and Aaron Ott."

"How many riders do your four outfits have?"

"Just the men that live here," Ellis said. "No drover would work for us. Altogether, there are five of us — Dade Tovar, Aaron Ott, Reuben and Andy Gilman, and me."

"A nice little crew," Trent said, fighting the despair that washed over him. "How about a deal? I'll ramrod your drive to market in exchange for a share of your profits."

Ellis spread his hands. "We can't get past the S Bar."

"I know a few tricks," Trent said. "Before I settled in the Nebraska sandhills, I went up the old Western Trail to Dodge three years; ramrodded an outfit the last year. I figure we've got a chance of getting the cattle out — it's worth a try, anyway."

Ellis nodded, enthusiasm coming slowly into his eyes. "I'll call the others here tomorrow. S Bar will have us outnumbered two to one even if we all stick together. But if you'll boss it, I'll take a chance."

Trent slept till the middle of the morning the next day. When he finally came out of his room, he found that Bill Ellis was back from his ride to his neighbors' ranches. He told Trent they'd meet that night.

Aaron Ott and his wife were the first to arrive. He was a tall, skinny man with sandy hair and pale blue eyes. His wife was short and dark. The Gilmans came next. Trent had already seen Beth and Andy Gilman, but their parents presented a contrast he wouldn't forget. Reuben Gilman was a big man, six feet tall and stockily built. He had brown, unruly hair and a temper to match, Trent guessed, as he heard him voice his opinions of the happenings in the country. Sarah Gilman was a tiny woman with dark hair and eyes and a rich, olive skin. She had obviously been a dazzling beauty in her younger days, for she still retained much of it.

The last to arrive were Dade Tovar and his sister, Zola. Dade was a short, heavy-set man with green eyes that Trent didn't like. But Ellis had said he was an expert cattle-man, and Trent would need men like that if they made the drive.

Dade's sister was a complete contrast to her brother. She was so tiny that Trent at first mistook her for a child. Barely five feet tall, and weighing less than a hundred pounds, she wore her red hair in two pigtails like a little girl. Trent wondered if her temper might not match the blaze of her hair.

"Let's get down to business," Reuben Gilman said gruffly when the Tovars had found seats.

Bill Ellis took the floor and explained Trent's plan to drive their cattle out to the market at Trail City in Colorado.

"It's only a little over two hundred miles. Trent thinks we can get the cattle there in good flesh," Ellis finished.

"If we can get them there at all," Tovar said. "Between us and the trail north is the S Bar."

"It's not going to be a picnic," Trent said. "But you're going to lose everything to the S Bar if you just sit here."

"We've got families to consider," Aaron Ott put in.

"Considering how few we are," Trent said, "we'll either all go or nobody will start."

"I'm moving out of this country, anyway," Tovar said. "I vote we try to take our cattle with us."

"What about your sister?" Trent asked.

"She'll go with us," Tovar said. "She'll drive our wagon, and I'll drive cattle."

Trent didn't like the idea of having a woman along. This was going to be more like a battle than a cattle drive. But if Tovar was determined to move out, this would be his best chance to do it.

"We'd like to move out, too," Beth Gilman said.

"We're not running scared!" Reuben shouted instantly. "I vote to take my cattle out to market. I've got to have the money to live on, but I'm not going to be run out by the Sparks."

"I vote to make the drive," Aaron Ott said hesitantly. "Like Reuben, I've got to have the money to live on."

"I guess that does it," Ellis said. "Mrs. Ott, why don't you move over here with my wife while we're gone? I don't like to leave her alone, and I doubt if Aaron wants you to stay alone, either."

It was quickly agreed that Mrs. Ott would move in with Mrs. Ellis. Mrs. Gilman would have Beth to help her keep the ranch running. And Zola Tovar was going on the drive.

"We'll start the roundup tomorrow," Trent said. "We'll gather the herd here in the valley below Bill's corrals. How long do you figure it will take?"

"Not long," Aaron Ott said.

"What do you have for law around here?" Trent asked Ellis after the last of the visitors had gone.

"Not much that's any good," Ellis said. "There's a deputy sheriff in town, but he plays his cards to win, which means he sees things Ira Spark's way."

"We'll have to do without the law's help then," Trent said grimly. "How many days do you figure it will take to get the cattle rounded up?"

"Four or five days ought to do it, unless some of us try to get our cattle back from the S Bar."

"Do you mean some of your stuff has strayed?" Trent asked, frowning.

"Strayed is a nice word for it," Ellis said.

Trent sighed. This was a big land, a land for big ranches and big men. To the west was the huge XIT ranch with three million acres. It was probably the existence of that big ranch that drove men like Ira Spark to try to get a grip on huge chunks of this land themselves.

Trent rode out with Bill Ellis the next morning to drive in his cattle. There were a few fences but they were in bad repair, and cattle of several brands were on the prairie.

"EX is my brand," Ellis said. "That circle around a small diamond is Gilman's, the up-sidedown T is Tovar's, and the OT brand is Aaron Ott's."

"Plenty of S Bar stuff here, too," Trent said. "Why doesn't Spark keep his cattle on his own range? He's got plenty."

"He claims this, too, remember?" Ellis said. "That's why he says these cattle of ours belong to him — he said they've been getting fat on his grass."

"He has no legal right to it, does he?"

"Of course not. I doubt if he has legal right to ten per cent of the land he claims. But his guns say it's his, and guns talk louder than any argument we can put up."

By noon of the second day, Ellis had most of his cattle brought into the home corrals. He was short nearly thirty head.

"Where do you figure they are?" Trent asked.

"Mixed in with the S Bar stuff," Ellis replied.

"Let's go get them."

"We'd be shot for rustling," Ellis said. "We better be glad we've got all but thirty."

Trent ground his teeth. "You'd let him steal you blind and not lift a finger! I'm going to look for the rest of your cattle. Coming?"

Reluctantly, Ellis reined around and followed Trent as he galloped to the northeast toward the S Bar headquarters. They rode along the high ridges, looking for cattle. When they located a grazing herd, Trent angled toward it, Ellis at his heels.

Trent started working slowly through the

milling herd. He found two-dozen head of EX cattle among the S Bar stuff.

Trent cut two of the EX steers out of the herd and pushed them to the edge of the milling cattle.

"Hold these while I cut out the others," Trent said to Ellis.

"Watch it!" Ellis suddenly shouted. "We've got company."

Trent turned in his saddle and saw Ira and Cole Spark spurring toward them.

CHAPTER 4

Trent reined his horse out of the herd and stopped beside Bill Ellis, waiting for the Sparks.

"Luck's with us," Ellis said softly, and Trent turned to look behind him.

Aaron Ott and Andy Gilman were riding hard from the direction of Ellis's ranch. They pulled up just ahead of the Sparks.

"Your wife said she saw you riding this way," Ott explained. "We figured what was up. Any of my cattle or Gilman's in here?"

Trent nodded. "I saw a few."

Ira and Cole Spark yanked their horses to a halt a few feet from them.

"Rustling cattle now?" Ira yelled.

"We're cutting out some critters that strayed off their home range," Trent said.

"There are no strays here!" Ira shouted. "This is my range — and every critter on it is mine!"

"Not these," Trent said. He watched the two Sparks carefully. They had galloped in as though they were ready to shoot it out. But with the addition of Ott and Andy Gilman to Trent's forces, their anger had faded to the point where only words would be used.

Trent glanced at Ellis and nodded toward the herd, then turned back to Ira and Cole Spark.

"We are just cutting out Ellis's, Ott's, and Gilman's cattle."

"We hang cattle thieves here just like horse thieves!" Ira shouted.

"You might be putting your own neck in a noose," Trent warned. "We could claim you stole these cattle."

"How can a man steal his own cattle?"

"They're not yours," Trent snapped.

"They're mine! They've been eating my grass."

"Show me your deed to this land!"

Ira Spark's hand started toward his hip, then came back. "I'll give you ten minutes to get off my land," he yelled. "If you're not gone by then, I'll bring my men and we'll bury you right here."

Trent looked around. Ott was still at his side. Ellis and Andy were working the herd rapidly, cutting out the cattle that belonged to the little ranchers.

"Give us twenty minutes," Trent said, "and we'll be gone."

Cole Spark shouted wildly as Ellis and

Andy pushed more cattle out of the herd. "Pa, they're stealing our cattle!" His hand dropped to his gun butt.

Trent moved quickly, his gun appearing in his hand.

"Just keep the hardware cool," he warned. "The S Bar wouldn't be much good without its two bosses. You get unruly and that's how it will be."

Cole's hand pulled away from his gun and Ira sat his horse, swearing. Ellis and Andy finished the cutting and started the herd toward home. Trent motioned to the two Sparks.

"Head home and ride easy. Don't try using those rifles. We've got rifles, too, twice as many as you have right now."

Ira swore again and jerked his horse around. Cole followed him, neither looking back as they disappeared over the knoll.

Back at Ellis's, Trent suggested that Tovar, Gilman, and Ott bring the cattle they had gathered over to the valley below Ellis's corral. They would mount a guard around them tonight. Ira Spark wasn't likely to allow what had happened this afternoon to go by without retaliating.

"Ott and Gilman aren't done gathering," Ellis said.

"They don't want to lose what they have

gathered," Trent said. "We'll use this valley for a holding range."

Ott agreed, and he and Andy left, promising to bring their cattle over and to tell Dade Tovar to do the same.

By sundown, cattle wearing the Circle Diamond, the OT, and the upside-down T were streaming into the valley. It made a bigger herd than Trent had expected. Aaron Ott agreed to take the first watch over the herd, and Trent promised to stand the late watch.

After supper, Trent asked Bill a question that had been nagging at him. "Do you think Cole Spark would keep the money he stole from me on the S Bar?"

"Not likely," Ellis said. "He probably deposited it in the bank in town."

"How would he explain a windfall of three thousand dollars? Or would anybody get curious?"

Ellis shrugged. "He could say it was a down payment on the cattle he is to deliver this summer. Everybody knows he went north to locate a market for the S Bar beef."

"Did Fanok go with him?"

Ellis shook his head. "Fanok never showed up here till Cole came back. I don't know where he came from."

"Is there any way I can find out if Spark put that money in the bank?"

"I reckon there is," Ellis said. "The teller in the bank is a good friend of mine. He isn't supposed to reveal anything about deposits, but he'll tell me if I ask him."

"If it's in the bank, I suppose it's out of my reach," Trent said. "But if not, it probably means that Cole still has it somewhere. I'll get it out of him if I have to burn him to a crisp, inch by inch."

Ellis grinned. "I want to see that. Tomorrow we'll ride in to town and find out."

Nothing disturbed the newly formed herd in the valley during the night, and after breakfast the next morning, Trent rode in to town with Ellis. When the bank opened, Ellis went in and talked to the teller. Trent met him when he came out.

"What did he say?"

"He'll let us know at noon," Ellis said.

Ellis and Trent met the teller at the restaurant. The teller was a small, wiry man with beady eyes. He glanced at Trent, but Ellis nodded his head.

"He's the one Cole stole the money from," he explained.

"Cole didn't deposit any money in the bank," the teller said. "In fact, both Cole and Ira Spark are pretty low on cash. If Cole had three thousand dollars, I'm sure he would have deposited it."

Ellis thanked the teller and, when he was gone, turned to Trent. "Well, there goes that theory."

"I'm glad it's not in the bank," Trent said. "But I wonder where he's keeping it. Maybe Fanok has it."

"Didn't you say something about a girl?" Ellis asked.

Trent nodded. "I distinctly remember hearing a woman telling them to hurry after they had knocked me down and were taking my money belt. They might have left the money with her at Trail City. They could get it when they take their cattle north this summer."

Ellis nodded thoughtfully. "That seems reasonable."

"I'll check it out when I get to Trail City," Trent agreed, "if I don't get a chance to burn the truth out of Cole Spark or Fanok before then."

"Look who's coming," Ellis said.

Trent wheeled, expecting to see Cole Spark and half the S Bar crew.

But it was Dade Tovar and Zola coming in a buggy, with Dade's horse tied behind. Riding beside the buggy was Andy Gilman.

"They don't seem to be rounding up cattle any faster than we are," Ellis said, striding to meet them.

Trent followed Ellis and was in front of the harness shop when Tovar pulled the buggy into the hitchrack.

"Broke the rigging on my saddle," Tovar explained. "Had to bring it in to get it fixed. Need some harness work done before we start north, so I brought that in, too."

"I've got to get a new rope," Andy put in. "Caught mine so often on wire fences that it's frayed out."

"Better get it done and get back to work," Ellis said. "We can't afford to waste time."

"I need some things from the store," Zola said as she reached for Trent's hand. "I wasn't expecting the pleasure of meeting you here. Will you have time to help me do my trading?"

Trent shot a glance at Ellis. "I reckon."

He discovered that she needed his help like the ocean needed rain, but she kept him at her side and he enjoyed his chore. She chattered steadily about the things she was buying and her anticipation of the trip.

Trent kept still until she mentioned the trip north. "I hate to see you go north with the herd," he said. "It's liable to get rough. We're going to have trouble getting the cattle out, and you might get hurt."

"I'll take my chances," Zola said carelessly. "Anyway, I won't be afraid with you bossing the drive."

Trent shifted uneasily. Surely she wasn't foolish enough to think any one man could prevent trouble. Then he saw Dade Tovar and Andy Gilman at the door glaring at him.

Zola saw them, too, but she took Trent's hand possessively and led him to another counter, where she pointed to the bracelets and rings under the glass. Trent looked back at Tovar and Andy.

Zola finished her purchases and Trent helped her carry them to the buggy; then he turned toward the harness shop to see how Dade Tovar was making out. He found the saddle repaired, the workman already busy with a set of harness. But Trent forgot the leather work as Tovar caught his arm inside the shop, out of sight of the buggy.

"You let Zola alone," Tovar snapped.

"I was only doing what she asked me," Trent said, his anger rising. "Anyway, Zola is old enough to decide who she wants for her friends."

"I'm still deciding it for her," Tovar said sharply. "You stay away from her until we know you better."

"You're going to find out some things about me in a hurry if you keep prodding me," Trent warned, yanking his arm away.

He wheeled out of the shop and strode down to the hitchrack in front of the restaurant where he had left his horse. Ellis had already ridden out of town.

Trent spurred down the street, sighting Ellis ahead of him. But before he caught up with him, he heard a horse drumming the trail behind and twisted in the saddle. He again expected to see Cole Spark or a small army of S Bar riders, but this time it was Andy Gilman. Trent reined down to a walk to let Andy catch up.

"You let Zola alone!" Andy shouted before he reached Trent.

Trent scowled. This subject was beginning to rub him raw. "You'd better have a good reason for telling me what to do," he said testily. "What Zola and I do is none of your business."

Andy's face colored. Trent was sure it was only partly from anger. "Zola is a fine girl. She comes from the East. She doesn't understand men like you."

"She understands plenty," Trent said positively. "Anyway, we've got a bigger job to do than fight over a girl."

Trent spurred his horse into a gallop again, shortening the distance between him and Ellis. There were some things he didn't understand about this afternoon. Zola Tovar was far from being as naïve as she pretended to be. And why had her brother been so upset over Zola's attentions to him? And now Andy. But Andy was no mystery to Trent. Although two or three years older than his sister, Andy was far less mature. He was more like a schoolboy. And now he had a schoolboy crush on Zola Tovar. He didn't want Trent spoiling it for him.

They had just caught up with Bill Ellis, and Trent had reined his horse down to a pace matching Ellis's, when Andy, apparently forgetting his anger at Trent, stood up in his stirrups and pointed ahead.

"Hey, there comes Sis. And she's riding like her saddle was afire."

Trent touched his horse into a gallop, and Ellis and Andy kept pace with him. They reined up as Beth came to a skidding halt.

"It's Pa!" she screamed. "He's gone after Cole Spark with a gun!"

"Why?" Trent demanded.

"Cole came over and took some of our cattle. Claimed they were his. Pa was so mad he couldn't talk. When Cole left, he ran back in the house and got his gun, then saddled up and took after Cole."

"He'll be killed," Ellis said flatly. "Which way did they go?"

"Toward the S Bar. Hurry! Maybe we can stop him."

"I doubt it," Ellis said, "but we'll try. Lead off; we'll follow."

CHAPTER 5

Trent didn't know how much of a gun fighter Reuben was, but he'd guess none at all. Cole Spark was a gun fighter. Their one hope to keep Reuben Gilman alive was to get to him before he overtook Cole Spark and challenged him.

Trent wondered if this wasn't just the start of trouble for the small ranchers. Counting Trent, they had only six men. Enough, perhaps, to handle the size of herd they would put on the trail, but if something happened to some of those men, what would they do?

"How far?" Trent yelled as they drove their horses ahead.

"We'll cut him off in another mile," Beth yelled back.

Trent saw the tightness of her face as she urged her horse on. But even that couldn't hide the soft mold of her cheeks and chin or the smooth curve of her mouth.

Ellis pointed ahead. Trent saw the small bunch of cattle going slowly up a knoll with a man riding behind them. And two hundred yards behind him was another rider, coming hard.

Even as they looked, the rider in the rear slowed his horse and threw up a rifle. The echo of the rifle rolled across the hills.

"Stop him! Stop him!" Beth screamed, and kicked her horse harder.

But they were too far away. The rider pushing the cattle wheeled in the saddle as the rifle spanged again. He dived off his horse and, for a moment, Trent thought that Reuben had been lucky with his shot.

But then he saw that Cole Spark was pulling his rifle from its boot. Holding the reins of his horse over his arm, Spark knelt and took careful aim. Reuben fired again, but still from the saddle.

Then Spark's rifle belched smoke, and Reuben dropped his rifle and clutched the horn of his saddle. The horse shied as his rider slid to one side of the saddle. Then Reuben released his grip on the saddle horn and slid to the ground, the horse side-stepping away, reins dragging.

Cole Spark remounted, slid his rifle into its boot, and turned toward the cattle again. If he noticed them, he gave no sign of it.

Trent and Ellis spurred toward the fallen man. When Trent looked at Reuben, he knew there was nothing anybody could do.

Cole Spark's aim had been dead center.

"Let's go get him," Andy said savagely.

"Won't do any good," Ellis said, "unless we kill him. If we do that, we'll all be hanged for murder."

"He murdered Pa!" Beth said between sobs.

Ellis sighed. "I know. But the law here won't convict a Spark for that."

"We'll give the law a chance," Trent said. "Make the sheriff cook up some story to get Spark off free. At least, we'll show the people here that the law is all a farce."

"I reckon they know that already," Ellis said.

"We've got to do something," Andy said.

"All right," Ellis agreed. "Come on, Jason. This is our job."

Trent nodded. "Andy, take Beth home. We'll send somebody out from town to get your pa."

Trent expected to have to ride into the S Bar yard to get Cole Spark. Surely he had seen them, and he wouldn't stay to fight them alone. But when they got over the hill, Trent saw Spark still pushing the small herd toward the S Bar headquarters.

"What do you make of it?" he asked.

"Beats me," Ellis said. "Unless he's so sure nothing can happen to him that he's showing us how useless it really is to fight the S Bar."

"How can he be sure that we won't plug him when we catch up with him?" Trent said. "Dead roosters don't crow."

"Would you shoot him if he didn't show any fight?"

"I reckon not."

"He knows the kind of people he's dealing with. Reuben Gilman and maybe Dade Tovar are the only ones over here who would shoot before they were shot at."

Trent spurred his horse forward, not certain that he wouldn't shoot first. Remembering the grief on Beth Gilman's face when he had left her weeping beside the body of her father brought out in him the urge to kill.

He moved ahead of Ellis, and when he came within fifty yards of Cole Spark, the S Bar man turned toward him, halting his horse. He lifted his hands shoulder-high and waited. Trent's fingers relaxed their grip on his gun; he couldn't shoot a man who had his hands in the air.

Trent reined up in front of Spark, and Ellis came up beside him. Spark wasn't even wearing a gun belt, and his rifle was fastened in its boot.

"Where's your gun?" Trent demanded.

"In my saddlebag," Spark said. "I was afraid I'd run into trouble when I went after our cattle so I put it there to avoid trouble. I didn't think the old fool would fight an unarmed man."

"You knew he would," Ellis snapped. "Anyway, according to Beth, you weren't so peace-loving when you came to the Circle Diamond."

Trent turned toward the cattle. He saw a half-dozen S Bar cattle there, but most of them carried the Circle Diamond brand.

"You were stealing his cattle," Trent said grimly. "Reuben had a right to shoot you whether you had a gun or not."

"I was going after my own cattle," Spark snapped. "Look at the S Bar brand."

"They weren't on the Circle Diamond," Ellis retorted.

"Prove it," Spark said. "I say they were there. I went after them and some of Gilman's cattle drifted in. I haven't had time to cut them out."

In spite of the flimsiness of the story, Trent had a feeling Spark would stick to it and get away with it. Still, all he and Ellis could do was take him in to town and have the deputy sheriff put him in jail.

"Start on with him," Ellis said. "I'll turn back Gilman's cows, then catch up with you."

In town, Trent and Ellis signed a statement saying they had seen Cole Spark shoot Reuben Gilman. The deputy scowled at them, but he put Spark in a jail cell. Spark was as unconcerned as if he were being treated to a dinner in the hotel.

"He'll be out before we get home," Ellis predicted as they rode out of town.

Trent didn't argue. If it came to a trial, not even he or Ellis could say that Reuben hadn't fired the first shot. It would be a case of self-defense. The real crime had been Spark's running off Reuben's cattle. And that could never be proved here, where the power behind the law was Ira Spark.

Trent and Ellis had notified the undertaker, and he had gone out after Reuben's body. The funeral was scheduled for the next afternoon. Trent considered staying with the cattle that were being held in the valley below Ellis's corrals. He wouldn't put it past the S Bar to raid that herd while everybody was at the funeral. But Ellis convinced him that not even Ira Spark would stoop that low.

The funeral service was short. Trent found it hard to keep his mind on the preacher's words. His crew was one man short now. He'd have only four men besides himself. Maybe even Andy would back out now that he didn't have his father to lean on or to drive him.

After service, the funeral procession led to the little cemetery south of town. Trent tried to hide his surprise when he saw Cole Spark in the procession. He wasn't as surprised that he was out of jail as he was that he was at the funeral. It was just a show of defiance, he decided.

Vane Fanok was there, too, but his face showed something akin to real concern. After the last words had been said at the graveside, Fanok approached Beth and said something to her. Trent wondered if the words of sympathy could possibly be sincere.

The funeral over, the little ranchers left town in a group, one buggy and three buckboards. Trent rode with Ellis. He wished he could think of something to say to Beth and Mrs. Gilman, but he was no good at finding the right thing to say when the choice of words was so important.

Ellis's ranch was the closest to town, and all the rigs stopped there at Mrs. Ellis's invitation. She went inside to bring out some cookies she had baked for the occasion. Trent saw that nothing had disturbed the grazing herd.

Then, just before the Gilmans, Otts, and

Tovars were ready to start for home, Beth spoke to Trent. Her eyes were red but dry, and determination hardened her jaw.

"We're going north with the herd," she announced.

Trent frowned. "We? You mean Andy, don't you?"

"All the Gilmans," Beth said. "You know, Ma and I were for moving when you first brought up this idea of driving our cattle north — only, Pa was against it. Well, Pa can't vote now. We're leaving here."

Trent thought of having two more women on the drive, and his heart sank. Reuben Gilman's killing only emphasized the lengths to which the S Bar would go to make sure these cattle didn't leave the valley.

"What does Andy say about it?" he asked.

"Doesn't make any difference," Beth said flatly. "Ma and I vote to go, and we're going. Anyway, you're going to be shorthanded now, and I can make as good a hand as Pa would have."

"But you're a woman!"

"That's no crime," Beth snapped.

Trent was jolted by the sharpness of her voice. "I'm glad you are," he said hastily, then realized that the more he said, the deeper into trouble he was going to get. "Where will you go?"

"To the Nebraska sandhills. You said there was land up there still to be had for the taking."

"I reckon," Trent admitted, wishing he had kept his mouth shut about his ranch. He couldn't accept the responsibility of three women on this drive. And yet, how was he going to avoid it?

He wondered if any of them would see Nebraska — or even Trail City, for that matter — less than half the distance to the Nebraska sandhills.

CHAPTER 6

The bedded-down herd spent another undis-turbed night, and Trent thought about the final days of preparation for the trail. There was bound to be more trouble before they pointed a hoof toward Trail City.

Leaving Bill Ellis to keep an eye on the herd, he rode to the Gilmans' to help Andy round up the last of the Circle Diamond cattle.

"We had almost all of them bunched up before Pa was killed," Andy said. "But they spread out the last couple of days."

"We'll push them over to Ellis's place as soon as we round them up this time," Trent said.

They weren't badly scattered and they hadn't wandered far. Trent was bringing in two he had found over a hill from the corral when he saw Vane Fanok reining up in front of the house.

"What's he doing here?" Trent asked Andy at the corral.

"Here to see Beth, I reckon," Andy said. "He's been here a couple of times before.

Now I reckon he's got a good excuse. Yesterday he made quite a fuss telling her how sorry he was that Pa got killed."

"I bet!" Trent growled. "I wouldn't believe him if he said he was hungry when I knew he'd been out of grub for a month."

"Shall we run him off?" Andy asked hopefully.

"Beth can take care of herself, I reckon," Trent said. "Let's get these cattle rounded up."

Before noon, all the cattle were in the corral, and Trent and Andy rode up to the house before starting the cattle toward Ellis's place.

"What did Fanok want here?" Andy asked when they dismounted.

"He came to tell us he was sorry about what happened," Mrs. Gilman said.

"He told you that yesterday," Andy said.

"He acted like he was really sorry," Beth said.

"Did you tell him you were going north with the herd?" Trent asked.

"Yes," Beth said. "Why shouldn't I?"

"What else did you tell him?" Trent countered.

Beth stopped her work at the stove and turned to face Trent, her hands on her hips.

"What business is that of yours?" she said sharply.

"That's what I'm trying to find out," Trent said. "I think he came over just to pry into our plans."

"That's not so," Beth retorted. "Can't you believe any good of anybody?"

"Not Vane Fanok," Trent said tightly. "Not when I know what kind of a snake he is."

Trent knew he was only feeding her anger, but he couldn't help giving vent to his feelings. He saw Beth's face flush, but she only bit her lower lip.

"I don't believe he's spying," she said finally, with forced calm. "But even if he is, that can work two ways. Wouldn't you like to know what the S Bar is up to? Vane Fanok should know."

Trent frowned. He didn't like the idea of Beth having anything to do with Fanok, but he had to admit there was sound logic in her argument. Fanok should know the plans of the S Bar and maybe Beth could pry the information out of him.

When Trent and Andy pushed the last of the Circle Diamond cattle into the herd on Ellis's place, he found all the others there, too. Bill Ellis rode out to meet them.

"This is it, Jason," he said. "We're about ready."

Trent nodded. "Two things left to do: put a trail brand on these critters and get our supplies."

Trent called the men together. "We'll pick a road brand and begin branding in the morning. Then we'll get our supplies from town and head out. Tovar, can you be ready to move that soon? How about you, Andy?"

They assured Trent that their women would have things ready to leave the valley for good by the time the herd was ready to go.

"What about a road brand?" Aaron Ott asked.

"You brand your cattle with an OT on the right shoulder," Trent said. "Why not brand all the others the same? When we get to Trail City it will be easy to separate them. Those with no other brand will be Ott's; the others can pick theirs by their own brand. It will save us the chore of branding any of Ott's cattle."

"He's got as many as anybody else, too," Bill Ellis said. "I vote for the OT road brand." The others agreed.

The work of branding was a dirty, slow business. Ellis's corrals weren't big or strong enough to hold the grown cows and steers, so the branding had to be done in the valley.

When the branding was almost done,

Trent called Ellis to one side. "We'd better take a wagon to town and get the supplies. We should be ready for the trail in a couple of days."

"Who's going to do the cooking for us?" Ellis asked.

"Beth has already agreed to," Trent said. "That will free one more man for riding. Mrs. Gilman and Zola Tovar will drive the family wagons. Every man will be needed to keep the herd moving."

"That's for sure," Ellis agreed. "Looks to me like Aaron, Dade, and Andy can finish the branding this afternoon by themselves. I'll get the wagon ready, and we'll drive in to town after dinner and get the supplies."

As soon as dinner was over, Trent and Bill Ellis hitched up to the wagon they had converted into a chuck wagon and drove in to town.

Trent hoped they could get to town and back without seeing any S Bar riders. But as soon as they reached the end of Main Street, he realized that they were not going to be so lucky. A half-dozen S Bar riders were in town, and Ira and Cole Spark were with them.

"Looks like trouble," Ellis said softly. "Shall we turn around and head for home?"

"Running scared never got anybody anything but a bullet in the back," Trent said.

The wagon rolled slowly up the street. Trent gripped the rifle in his lap. There might not be any need for it, but he didn't believe they'd let Ellis and him get out of town with any supplies.

Ira Spark led Cole and the half-dozen S Bar men out into the middle of the street to block the path of the wagon. Trent toyed with the idea of grabbing the reins from Ellis and slapping them, driving the team right through the men. But he knew that although they might cripple a few S Bar men, it wouldn't help get the little ranchers' cattle out of the valley.

"Expecting to buy a wagonload of something, Ellis?" Ira Spark asked.

"Figured on it," Ellis said. "Now get out of our way."

"The store hasn't got anything to sell to you!"

"I'll let the storekeeper tell me that," Ellis said.

Trent's fingers tightened on his rifle.

"Save you a lot of trouble if you just turn around and go home," Spark said.

"It might save you some trouble if you'd get out of the way and let us by," Trent said.

"Look around you, Trent," Cole Spark said, his hand resting on the butt of his gun. "Who do you think is going to be in trouble if you start something?"

Anger surged through Trent. "One thing you can count on, Cole: if trouble starts, you won't be around to celebrate the victory."

Cole scowled darkly but he made no move to press the argument. Ira Spark stepped in.

"Simmer down, now. No need to make a big thing of this." He looked at the people who were peering out from safe doorways and windows.

Trent guessed that Spark was holding back as much because of the impression that would be made as he was because of any fear of the outcome of a fight. S Bar controlled the country and the town but that control might not withstand the criticism a fight like this would stir up.

"All we're asking is to be let by," Ellis said.

"We'll let you by," Ira said. "But I want you to understand that you're not moving one head of stock out of this valley. Those cattle belong to me: you've been fattening them on my grass. You try taking one critter north and you'll be singing your own death chant."

"There'll be more funerals than just ours," Trent said, meeting Ira's stare. "A man can't get much satisfaction counting the profits from his stolen goods if half his family's in the grave."

Ira Spark glared at Trent. For a moment, Trent thought he was going to start the fight he had been trying to avoid. But Ira Spark just stood there.

"Go to the store and see what you get," Ira said thickly. "But remember, you've been warned — not one head of stock leaves this valley!"

Spark stepped out of the road and his men followed. Ellis slapped the reins, and the team moved on down the street toward Al Rose's store. Once they were past the men, Trent stole a quick look back. But the S Bar men were just standing, staring sullenly after the wagon.

"That was mighty close," Ellis said, wiping a hand across his forehead.

"Too close," Trent admitted. "But if we'd turned tail and run, we'd never have gotten our herd out."

"We won't, anyway, if Ira Spark can stop it."

"Maybe he can't," Trent said. "He doesn't have this town as completely under his thumb as we thought. He was worried about what people would think if he started a fight."

"Maybe," Ellis admitted. "But I won't feel easy until we get our supplies and get back to the ranch."

They wheeled the wagon into the hitch-rack in front of Al Rose's store and climbed out.

"This the only store in town?" Trent asked.

"Only one that carries enough supplies to outfit a trail drive," Ellis told him.

They crossed the porch and went inside. The store was a large one, but the shelves were almost bare. The man behind the counter was small, and his head was as bald as an egg, although he was not an old man — in his thirties, Trent guessed. His blue eyes were flashing dangerously.

"Store's closed, Bill," he said in a shrill voice.

"Closed?" Ellis echoed. "How come?"

"Nothing to sell," Rose said. "Look for yourself." He waved a hand at the empty shelves.

"But you always keep a big supply on hand," Ellis said.

"Sure I do," Rose said. "But the S Bar just cleaned me out."

Ellis leaned against the counter. "You mean Spark bought everything you had?"

"Everything that could be used on a trail drive," Rose said.

"Did he need that much?" Trent asked.

"No, he didn't," Rose said. "He took three

68

times as much as he'd need if he had thirty men, which he don't have." Rose was as mad as a hen tossed into a water trough.

"Looks like you made a good profit, anyway," Trent said.

"Looks that way," the storekeeper agreed. "But it ain't how it looks. Sure, the S Bar bought all my stuff. But do you know how they paid me? With a piece of paper that says they'll pay the cash when they get back from Trail City. I'd put every penny I had into supplies because I figured there was going to be some big drives out of this valley this spring. Now I'm out of business and not a penny to show for it. I can't buy any more till I get paid for what Spark took."

Ira Spark and his men were waiting on the street, and they watched in silence as Bill Ellis and Trent drove out. A mile out of town, Trent broke the silence.

"Drive past the S Bar. I want to see how near Spark's herd is ready to go."

"We'll get shot without ceremony if they catch us out here," Ellis said as they neared the S Bar.

"Maybe," Trent replied. "But they were in town and I reckon they figured on celebrating their victory before they came home." He pointed to a big herd south of the corrals. "Looks like they're about ready to travel. They've got all the supplies. What will their next move be?"

"Head north and leave us here to rot," Ellis said bitterly.

Trent shook his head. "I have a hunch they'll try to take the OT herd with them. The herd is already rounded up — what better time to drive it north?"

"You think they'll try to steal our herd?" Ellis asked.

"They want to get your cattle out of this valley, don't they?"

Ellis nodded slowly. "They might try that trick, at that."

Trent nodded. "Let's get home."

At Ellis's place, they found the other men finishing the job of branding the OT road brand on the trail herd. But when they saw the empty chuck wagon, they gathered around.

Ellis explained the trick Ira Spark had pulled, and Trent saw despair wash over the faces of the men.

"We expect the S Bar to try to run off the herd tonight so they can throw our stuff in with theirs and trail it all north," Trent said. "I've had enough of Spark's tricks for one day. We'll double our guard — I want every man to stay here tonight."

He sent Bill Ellis and Andy Gilman to ride

70

guard. There were four hundred head gathered on the meadow south of Ellis's buildings. If Trent had the supplies he needed, he'd be ready to start the herd north in another day.

Expecting the hours from ten to two to be the most likely ones for the S Bar to strike, Trent chose that shift for himself, Dade Tovar, and Aaron Ott.

Trent was just rousing Ott and Tovar for the second guard when he heard Andy yelling.

"They're coming!"

CHAPTER 7

Trent felt a fleeting moment of satisfaction that he had guessed right on Ira Spark's next move, but it was gone instantly. They had to stop the raiders or spend the next two days rounding up the cattle, and it was likely they would never recover most of the cattle — for they would be pushed into the big S Bar herd and vanish.

The relief horses were already saddled. The three men at the corral tightened the cinches and were mounted in less than a minute after Andy yelled. Trent led the way out toward the herd. He met Andy, who was pointing to the northwest.

"I was riding out that way to check a suspicious noise," Andy said. "And I heard horses' hoofs hitting rocks along the creek over there."

"We'll check it out," Trent said. "Bill, you stay with the herd. The rest of you come on."

The four galloped to the northwest and topped the rise. There they faced three surprised riders. The three jerked back on their reins so hard their horses reared.

Trent had his gun in his hand, but he yelled at the others, "Don't shoot unless you have to."

He led the charge down the slope at the three riders. For a moment they were so confused that that they neither ran nor fought. They had expected the little ranchers to be so discouraged that they wouldn't fight. One of them yelled and wheeled his horse, and the other two followed.

"Let's catch them," Andy yelled, and dug his heels into his horse's sides.

But Trent was satisfied to let them get away. If they caught the three raiders, or even got too close, there was bound to be gunplay. Even if no one got hurt, the noise might start the herd running. Bill Ellis was alone with the herd, and one man couldn't keep four hundred spooked cattle from running.

They followed the raiders for about a quarter of a mile, but then Trent held up a hand and reined up.

"They weren't expecting four of us to be on the welcoming committee," Tovar said.

"We still need supplies," Trent said. "Andy, you go get Bill and hit the sack. I doubt if we have any more trouble tonight."

They held a council the next morning, right after breakfast.

"Let's go north, anyway," Andy said. "We're ready. We can live on beef and water if we have to."

"Maybe we can get supplies at the first town we pass," Tovar said.

"We need things right now," Ott objected. "I was checking yesterday. We don't have enough axle grease to grease our three wagons once."

"I agree with Aaron," Ellis said. "We need supplies."

Trent saw the others were evenly divided in thinking. Andy Gilman and Dade Tovar, who were planning to move out of the valley for good, were both eager to get going — even if it meant starting without supplies. Bill Ellis and Aaron Ott, who planned to sell their cattle and return to their homes, wanted to make sure they were ready before they started.

"Looks like a split vote," Andy said. "You'll have to decide it, Trent."

"I'd like to get on the trail," Trent said, "but it's too risky to start without supplies. The S Bar is out to stop us any way they can."

"I can find out where the S Bar supplies are," Beth said. "Two can play at their game." The vote to steal the supplies from the Sparks was unanimous.

★ ★ ★

The next day Zola laid a hand on Trent's shoulder as he crouched to screw the nut back on the axle. "You'll find a way out for us if one can be found. I like a man who is resourceful."

Trent looked up at Zola. Tiny, she would barely come to his shoulder if he stood up. She was pretty, too — he didn't deny it. But he didn't respond to her advance. He knew the reason was up there in the house now with Mrs. Ellis and Mrs. Gilman.

"We'll find a way to get out of here if we can," he said.

"Getting there isn't going to be half the fun of making the trip," Zola said, and Trent didn't miss her meaning.

"It won't all be fun," he said. "The Sparks aren't going to just sit back and let us go."

He finished the wheel and stood up. Zola didn't move away but stood gazing up into his face with a look that a man would have to be blind not to understand. He recalled how Zola had clung to him in the store in town and how both Dade Tovar and Andy had reacted. Dissension like that was something he didn't need among the men. They had to be of one mind and move with one effort if they hoped to get this herd out of Texas.

75

As soon as he could find an excuse, he got away and Zola went back to the house. But he had been too late in making his escape. Andy strode over to him as he was checking his equipment for the second time.

"Shining up to Zola again, I see," Andy said through clenched teeth.

"I wasn't doing the shining," Trent said. "You act like a kid in knee pants with your first love affair."

"I told you to let Zola alone," Andy repeated.

Trent turned to face Andy squarely. "Look, Andy, you're supposed to be a grown man. If you want a girl, go after her. But don't come around crying like a spoiled brat if you're not man enough to get her."

For a moment, Trent thought Andy was going to swing at him, but instead, he wheeled and strode away.

About half an hour later, Trent saw Zola with Andy, and she was giving him the same warm treatment. The fact that she was flirting with Andy didn't make him jealous, but it did whip up more misgivings. Andy would think that Zola was his for the taking, and he'd be fighting mad if he caught her making eyes at Trent again. And she would flirt with Trent the next chance she got.

Just before sundown, Beth came out of the

house and walked down toward Trent at the corral. He saw her coming and thought of Zola. He wouldn't get a repeat performance of Zola's act, that was sure.

"I found out where the S Bar stored the supplies they took from Mr. Rose's store," she announced matter-of-factly.

"Good," Trent said in surprise. "Are they in a place where we can get to them?"

"It will be easy to get them. They're in that shed they use for a grain bin north of their barn and corrals."

Trent rubbed his chin, suspicion tugging at him. "That would be one of the easiest places on the ranch to sneak into. How did you find out the supplies were there?"

"Vane Fanok came over today. He was at our place for dinner. I pried the information out of him."

Trent nodded. "Maybe he had the information all ready to be pried out."

Beth's eyes snapped. "It's no trap, if that's what you think. He has no idea he gave me any information."

"We'll go after them," he said finally. "If we get what we need, we'll pay Rose cash for what we take."

Trent called the other men over, and Beth explained what she had found out about the supplies.

"We're going after those supplies," Trent said when Beth had finished. "I'll take Bill with me. The rest of you stay with the herd. Andy, you and Aaron take that canvas cover off the chuck wagon. It's going to be cloudy tonight, but that canvas top will still be easy to see. Andy, can we use your team of black horses?"

"Sure," Andy said.

"I'm coming with you," Beth said flatly. "I know the layout on the S Bar as well or better than Bill does. Anyway, you'll need a lookout while you two load the supplies."

Trent didn't want Beth to go, but he knew that she was more dependable than most of the men in the crew.

"We'll leave about ten," Trent said. "That should get us to the S Bar after everybody has gone to bed."

After supper, while they were preparing for the raid, Bill Ellis looked nervously off in the direction of the S Bar. "They may have guards out, you know."

Trent nodded. "Sure, I know. Got any better ideas?"

"No. Beth is positive Fanok didn't realize that he'd told any secrets. Well, let's hope everything works out."

The clouds rolled in even heavier than Trent had anticipated. The moon wasn't quite at first quarter, and they waited until after it had set before starting. There was practically no light on the prairie as Trent and Ellis moved out with the wagon. Beth had decided to ride her little black pony rather than the wagon. If Trent and Ellis got into trouble she could come back to Ellis's place for help.

In a swale a half mile from the S Bar, Trent reined up. "You say the shed is on this side of the other buildings?" he asked.

Ellis nodded. "Close to the corrals."

"If they're not guarding it, we shouldn't have much trouble," Trent said.

He moved the team out at a walk. They made little noise, only the squeak of the harness and an occasional squeal from the seat on the wagon.

They were almost to the corrals before Trent saw the big barn loom out of the darkness on the far side of the corrals. Then he saw the shed on the near side of the corrals. He pointed to it, and Ellis nodded silently.

Trent eased the wagon over behind it, one hand on the reins, the other gripping the rifle in his lap. If the place was guarded, they'd know it soon.

"The door is on the other side," Beth whispered. "I'll hold the team."

But before stepping out into the yard to reach the door, Trent paused at the corner of the building and looked into the S Bar yard. It was dark, but he could see enough to remember the place. He'd been near this spot that day Cole Spark had stepped around the corner of the house with his gun drawn.

But there was no light in the house and no sign of life anywhere around. Trent led the way to the bin door. It was a flimsy door but it was locked. Ellis hurried back to the wagon for a crowbar. A quick wrench with the crowbar, and the lock on the door snapped open.

Trent looked at the house but no lights came on. The bunkhouse was at right angles from the house and was even farther away from the bin.

Stepping inside the bin, Trent lit a match and cupped it in his hand. Beth had been right; the bin was nearly half full of every kind of supplies a trail outfit could use.

"Let's get what we need and get out of here," Ellis said nervously. "I feel like I'm looking down the barrel of a forty-four."

"Two of us," Trent admitted, and reached for a barrel of flour.

They had loaded two barrels of flour, some axle grease, and a side of salt pork when Beth ran to the door. Trent was searching for ammunition.

"Somebody's coming," Beth whispered.

"This is no place for a fight," Ellis whispered, peering out the door.

"We're not picking the place," Trent said. "We'd better watch the team."

"I'll watch the horses," Beth said, and disappeared around the corner of the shed.

Trent stepped outside. Beth hadn't said where the company was coming from, but he soon located him. Trent didn't relax, but he changed his strategy. He had been afraid they had been discovered by someone at the house or bunkhouse, but this was a rider heading toward the corral from town.

Trent pushed Ellis back inside. "Maybe he won't see us," he whispered.

"He's sure to see the team and wagon behind the shed," Ellis whispered back.

"Maybe not. It's pretty dark, and he doesn't act like he's got night raiders on his mind."

The man whistled tunelessly as he reined up at the corral gate. Trent and Ellis had their guns trained on him as he dismounted and unsaddled his horse. He pulled off the bridle, turned the horse into the corral, and walked toward the bunkhouse.

"He must have had a big night," Ellis whispered finally, breathing hard.

"We can thank some girl in town for keeping his mind occupied," Trent said. "Let's get this job finished."

Trent and Ellis went back to work loading the supplies. Trent found the ammunition stacked in large boxes. He was tempted to take it all, but time was important, and they couldn't carry more things on the drive than they would need. Extra ammunition would be as much of a burden as too much of anything else.

Twenty minutes later, they shut the door of the bin, mounted the wagon, and drove away.

At Ellis's the next morning, they inventoried their supplies.

"Let's ride in to town and settle up with Rose for this," Trent said.

Al Rose was surprised to see Trent and Ellis swing down in front of his store.

"I still ain't got nothing for sale," he told them.

"We're not here to buy anything," Trent said.

"Just to pay you for some of the things we did buy."

Rose frowned. "Quit talking in riddles. You ain't bought nothing, and you're not going to, because I ain't got nothing to sell."

"We just bought this list of things," Ellis said, and put the inventory they had made on the counter. "We helped ourselves last night from their cache," Trent said. "We figured the stuff was really yours since the S Bar hadn't paid for it so we're here to pay you cash for what we got."

Rose's face lit up. "Wish you'd taken it all."

"We couldn't have paid for that much," Ellis said.

"I'd love to see old Ira's face when he finds out what you've done," Rose said as he picked up the money.

The rest of the day was busy. Although they had already taken a day or two longer in preparation for starting than they had planned, there were a lot of last-minute details to attend to. But by late afternoon, the herd and the men were ready.

He could feel the tension in each of them as they prepared to move out. In Bill Ellis and Aaron Ott, there was a pessimistic, almost fatalistic attitude. Neither expected to get the cattle out of the valley, but each felt he had to try.

Tovar and Andy Gilman were more optimistic. They didn't expect to get by without a fight, but both expected to get their cattle to Trail City without too great a loss.

Trent wasn't as optimistic as Andy and Tovar. He was sure it would take both wits and guns to get past the S Bar.

The sun was an hour high when Andy spotted a visitor coming from town. Trent crossed the yard to meet the rider. Only when he got close did he recognize the storekeeper, Al Rose.

"What happened to you?" Trent demanded.

Rose was bloody and bruised, his face puffed and welted. But defiance flashed in the one eye that wasn't swelled completely shut.

"What does it look like?" he snapped. "I got beat half to death."

"Who did it?" Ellis asked, hurrying up beside Trent.

"Cole Spark and three S Bar hands."

"Why?" Trent demanded.

"They found out they'd been robbed of some of their supplies, and they figured I did it because they didn't pay cash. So they came in and beat me up."

Trent helped the storekeeper off his horse and to the house, where he hunched down against the wall. "What did they say when they didn't find the supplies?" Trent asked.

"Pounded me till I had to tell them what I knew about it."

84

"Which means they'll come here after the supplies," Ellis said.

"That's exactly how I figure it," Rose said. "Cole even made the remark that they'd get the stuff back. That's why I came out here. I thought if you knew they were coming, you might punch holes in their plans — or in them."

"How would you like to go north with our herd, Rose?" Trent asked. "We're short a man now that Reuben Gilman is dead."

Rose looked up, a gleam in his eye. "Keep talking."

"Not much more to say," Trent said. "The pay will be standard, providing you can do a man's work. It could get pretty hot if the Sparks live up to their threats."

"You just convinced me," Rose said. "If I can get a crack at the Sparks without having to do it alone, I'm all for it."

"Can you ride and rope?"

Rose shook his head. "I'm no cowboy. But I am a first-class cook."

Trent was about to say that Beth would do the cooking when Beth spoke up from the doorway.

"He's just the man we need. If Mr. Rose can drive the chuck wagon and do the cooking, Mama and Zola can do the camp chores. I'll make a hand with the herd — I can do that as well as any man."

Trent doubted if she could do what any man could do, but he didn't doubt her determination, and he didn't doubt that she'd make a first-class drover.

"How about it, Rose?" he asked.

"Count me in," Rose said. "I can drive a team all right. And nobody will go hungry, providing you keep the S Bar from stealing your supplies."

"We'll do something about that right now," Trent said.

"Better haul the wagon in by the house where we can guard it," Ellis said.

Trent nodded. "I've got another idea, too. I'd like to make them show their hand. You've got that old wagon over there that we're not taking on the drive. It will take only a few minutes to rig up a top on it so it would look like a chuck wagon in the dark. Let's set it out there for them to search. We'll put the wagon with the supplies up here between the house and the corrals."

The other men quickly agreed to the scheme. They fell to the task of rigging up the fake chuck wagon, and, before dark, pulled it out beyond Tovar's and Gilman's two loaded wagons. As darkness settled down, the wagon lost the giveaway signs that it was not ready for the trail. A sliver of a moon put enough light down from the western half of the sky to point it out but not show up any details.

Two were put on guard with the herd, and the rest tried to sleep. It was after ten when Andy sounded a cautious alarm.

Dade Tovar and Aaron Ott were out with the herd, but Trent and Ellis were in the house. Al Rose went to the window to see what was going on. Trent, Andy, and Ellis hurried out to the barn where they had their horses saddled.

"Wait and see what they do," Trent said. "If they start any trouble, we'll surprise them."

Several figures neared the wagon. Trent thought he could count four, but it was too dark to tell. The moon was almost down, and its light wasn't bright enough to reveal anything at a distance.

"Maybe we ought to get closer," Andy suggested.

"They'll only be fifty yards from us when they get to the wagon," Trent said. "If we move out of the shadow of the barn, they'll see us, and that will bring on a fight or scare them away."

Trent guessed the raiders had a wagon over the hill. Perhaps the men planned to carry the supplies out to the wagon to keep from waking anybody.

Trent saw four of them. One climbed into the wagon and a moment later stuck his head out. His muffled curses could be heard at the barn.

Andy laughed, and Trent and Ellis joined in. Trent could imagine their fury.

"What are they doing now?" Ellis asked.

The man who had been in the wagon had climbed out, and Trent saw two of them scurrying toward the wagons loaded with Tovar's and Gilman's things. Then he heard one of the men shout softly.

"Fire the all!"

"They're going to burn them!" Andy shouted.

"They just think they are," Trent said. "Let's go!"

He swung into the saddle and, with a yell, spurred his horse out into the open. There was a chorus of surprised shouts and curses as the S Bar men realized they had been caught. They ran frantically. Shots echoed through the night as they fired wildly at their pursuers.

"Don't shoot at them," Trent shouted, fighting an impulse to do it, himself.

He fired two shots into the ground behind the running men, then reined up as they disappeared over the rise.

"We'd better get to bed now," Trent said to the shaken group. "We'll leave one man to keep watch just in case they should come back."

Trent rose at daybreak to get things ready to hit the trail. Teams were hitched to the three wagons. Mrs. Gilman took her place on the wagon, and Zola Tovar handled the reins on the Tovar wagon.

Al Rose, one eye still swollen almost shut, took his place on the seat of the chuck wagon, a rifle leaning against the dashboard at his feet. Beth's horse was saddled and she waited with the men for Trent to assign her a place on the herd.

Trent had a sorry-looking outfit compared to the crews he had ramrodded up from Texas over the Dodge City trail. But this was a small herd, numbering only four hundred, while the others had been as high as three thousand.

"Bill, you and Andy ride point," Trent said. "You know how to get this herd out of here. Keep out of sight of the S Bar buildings. Ott, you and Beth ride flank; Tovar and I will bring up the drag."

Trent rode forward on the S Bar side of the herd, looking in the direction of the big ranch headquarters. He'd wager dollars against the holes in doughnuts that Ira and

Cole Spark wouldn't let this herd move peacefully out of the valley.

A mile dropped behind, then another. Still, there was no sign that the S Bar was aware that the OT herd was moving. By ten o'clock they had crossed the northern boundary of the S Bar range.

"Maybe they've decided to let us go," Andy said.

Trent shook his head. "Not Ira Spark."

"Maybe they haven't discovered we're moving," Tovar suggested.

Again, Trent shook his head. "They know, all right. They've got some other scheme up their sleeve. I'd give an eyetooth to know what it is."

Noon came and still there was no sign of trouble. Trent didn't share the optimism that was seeping into some of the others. He knew Ira and Cole Spark wouldn't give up easily — and nothing had happened to discourage them from trying to get their hands on these cattle.

At midafternoon, Trent saw a low cloud of dust hanging over the back trail. He turned his horse and galloped back. Halfway to their morning's starting point, he saw the big herd strung out for over a mile: the S Bar was on the move.

Then he understood the Sparks's strategy.

That huge herd could swallow up the four hundred OT cattle in one gulp anytime the two herds got together. There would be enough S Bar gunmen with that herd to make sure the OT men didn't get one head of stock back.

It was a simple plan. Ira Spark had let the little ranchers do all the work of rounding up the cattle and getting them on the trail. Then, somewhere between here and Trail City, he planned to take over.

Trent rode back and told the others that the S Bar herd was right behind them. He said nothing about his conclusion as to the reason it was there. But he did put a double guard over the herd when they bedded down for the night.

The night passed peacefully, and Trent wondered if Ira Spark would be content to let the OT herd alone until it was closer to its destination before trying to swallow it up.

But that hope vanished the second night about midnight when Andy, riding night guard, spurred toward the wagons screaming, "Stampede!"

CHAPTER 8

Andy's scream pierced Trent's slumber like the fiery jab of a bullet. He jerked upright, ripping away the cobwebs of sleep. He could hear the low rumble in the echo of Andy's yell. There was no mistaking it — he had heard it too often.

He kicked out of his blanket, pulling on his boots. "Where's Bill?"

But Andy didn't hear. He rode on toward the chuck wagon, yelling, "Stampede! Stampede!"

Al Rose stuck his head out from under the wagon. "We heard you the first time!" he yelled back.

Ott came from his bedroll, carrying one boot. He didn't have his hat or his gun.

"Mount up!" Trent yelled at Tovar and Ott. He buckled on his gun and turned to run toward the picket rope where the night horses were tied. The others were hobbled farther out. Trent couldn't spare another man to night-herd the horses.

Andy galloped up to Trent as he ran toward the horses. "They're running crazy," he shouted.

"Where's Bill?" Trent asked.

Andy waved wildly toward the sound of the rumble. "Out there."

"Well, get out there and help him turn those cattle!" Trent yelled.

If Andy had been a fourteen-year-old flunky around camp, Trent wouldn't have been surprised to find him half-hysterical with fright. But a grown man like Andy! Andy had acted like a spoiled schoolboy when he'd found Zola talking to Trent; now he was acting like a scared kid.

Trent had tightened the cinch on his horse when Tovar and Ott ran up to him. Rose was behind them.

"I wasn't figuring on a night ride," Rose said, "so I undressed when I went to bed."

"Got your guns?" Trent asked.

"Sure," Ott said and jerked the cinch tight on his saddle.

Trent saw Beth running toward the horses.

"No, you don't!" he shouted, swinging into the saddle and reining toward her. "A stampede is no place for you."

"I'm one of the crew," Beth snapped. "I said I'd make a hand."

"At driving you can," Trent said. "But not turning a stampede. You go back to the wagon."

He reined his horse to the southwest, aiming at a point ahead of the herd. He had to get to the head of the running stream of frightened cattle.

As he rode, he tried to think of some reason for the cattle running. The night was crystal clear. Maybe a stray coyote had frightened one steer. Sometimes that was all it took to start a nervous herd running.

But these weren't nervous cattle. Coming from small herds on small ranches, they had never been as wild as cattle that saw a man only a few times a year. Trent had handled wild cattle on most of his big drives up the trail through Kansas.

But something had scared them. Trent saw the cattle now. They were running toward the southeast, almost directly over the trail they had covered today.

Trent wheeled his horse and tried to overtake the leaders. He thought he was close to the head of the herd. The dust wasn't too thick here; it would have been choking him if he'd been near the back.

The cattle were running along determinedly, but it wasn't the crazy fright that he'd usually seen in stampedes. He dug in his spurs. They were heading straight as an arrow toward the S Bar herd. If they got into that herd, Trent and his men would never get the cattle back without a gun battle.

Suddenly he saw open ground ahead. He was almost even with the leaders. He began pushing the leaders over by crowding his horse into them. Then he saw the flash of a gun ahead of him. It was Bill Ellis. Throwing his horse and gun into the battle, Trent helped Ellis shove the lead cattle out of their path and to the right.

As the leaders started to turn back into the herd, the dust thickened and Trent could scarcely get his breath. But the cattle weren't running any more, just trotting and walking in a wide circle. The night was filled with their weary bawling.

"Looks like we've got them whipped," Trent said when he rode past Ellis again. "What started them running?"

"About twenty head of cattle came in from the north," Ellis said, "running like they had wolves hanging on their tails."

"They must have been pushed into our herd."

"That's the way I figure it," Ellis agreed. "Look at the direction they came from. Stampeded our herd straight back toward the S Bar."

Trent nodded. "Did you get a look at the cattle that came at us? Were they S Bar?"

"Thunder, I didn't get a look at anything

except our own critters high-tailing it out of there."

"Better bed down right here for the rest of the night," Trent said. "We can't be over three or four miles from camp."

The other three men were there then, and they rode slowly around the herd until it bedded down. Trent tried to read the brands as he rode along but it was too dark.

He sent Ellis and Andy back to camp after the herd bedded down. Trent rode guard through the night. He wanted to see the brands on the cattle that had been run into the herd last night, and he wanted to get a count on the OT herd.

Trent sent Rose back when it became clear that the herd would remain quiet until morning. As soon as dawn came, he started examining brands and making a rough count. For half a circle of the herd, he saw no unfamiliar brand or strange cattle. Then he came to one big, wild-eyed steer that was on its feet watching him. By pushing in close enough to make the steer turn around, he discovered it was a slick, wearing no brand at all. Farther on, he found several more without brands.

Spark had left fifteen or twenty wild steers unbranded for the purpose of starting a stampede of the OT herd. If anything went wrong, no blame could be pinned on the S Bar. If the OT caused trouble trying to get their cattle back, the S Bar would claim self-defense.

Before Ellis and Andy reached the herd, Trent had made a quick count of the cattle. They were short over twenty head.

"We'll have to fan out and find these cattle," he said when Ellis and Andy came.

"What about you and Bill?" Andy asked.

"We'll go straight down our back trail," Trent said.

He knew he wasn't fooling anybody, but he wasn't going to come right out and say he expected to find the OT cattle in the S Bar herd. If the cattle had split off from the herd, they would be either to the southwest or southeast of the herd now.

"We won't get them," Ellis said after the men had split up and started on the search.

"I doubt it," Trent agreed. "But if we lock horns with the Sparks I don't want Andy or Tovar there. Andy's too hotheaded, and I haven't figured Tovar out yet."

"I know what you mean," Ellis said. "He's a loner. Sometimes I figure he's all right, and again, I don't know. One thing sure, he is a good man with cattle."

"They've spotted us," Ellis said as they neared the S Bar.

"They were looking for us," Trent said.

He reined up to wait and Ellis did the same. Trent wasn't surprised when he saw Ira and Cole Spark ride up.

"Looking for trouble?" Ira demanded.

"Looking for about twenty head of OT cattle," Trent said. "We had a stampede last night and about twenty head split off from the herd."

"What makes you think they came this way?" Cole asked.

"They were stampeded this direction. It won't take long to check and see if they're mixed in with yours."

"It would take a lot more time than you've got," Ira said.

"You're not cutting our herd!" Cole put in, leaning over the horn of his saddle.

"If it will relieve your mind any," Ira added smugly, "there are twenty-one head of cattle carrying the OT brand mixed in with the S Bar herd. They got there some-time during the night — we don't know how."

"Then we'll just cut them out and relieve you of the responsibility of trailing them," Trent said, and nudged his horse forward.

Ira Spark shifted the rifle across his lap until the muzzle was pointing at Trent. "You won't do any cutting of the S Bar herd. Those cattle belong to the S Bar. They're where they belong right now and they're going to stay there."

Fury swept over Trent but he knew he and Ellis wouldn't have a chance bucking the Sparks now. Ira Spark had his rifle at the ready, and there was Cole behind him. And back at the herd, ten men waited for a signal to join them.

"You can't sell the OT cattle when you get them to market," Trent said. "They're not wearing your brand."

Ira spoke like someone explaining a simple problem to a child. "One of my men has already filed the OT road brand. He can sell any of my cattle that are carrying that brand."

Trent saw that Ellis was about ready to tackle the odds, regardless of the outcome. But there had to be a better time to press their point.

"You'd better get back to what's left of your herd," Cole said impatiently.

"We'll go when we get our cattle," Ellis snapped.

"You'll go right now," Cole said, and dropped his hand to his gun.

"Get going," Ira put in, "unless you want to be buried right here and have your grave tramped over by twenty-five hundred head of cattle."

"Come on, Bill," Trent said softly. He saw where this was leading. Ira was hoping Ellis would give him the excuse to kill him.

"Are you going to let them get away with rustling?" Ellis demanded.

"Can you think of anything else to do?" Trent asked. "Dead men don't trail cattle to market."

"Smart thinking," Cole Spark said. "Now get out of our way. We're driving our cattle up this trail."

Trent fought an urge to smash his fist into Cole Spark's teeth. Only the promise to himself that someday he would do just that held his fury in check.

"Come on, Bill," he repeated, and wheeled his horse around.

Reluctantly, Ellis turned his horse and followed Trent back up the trail.

"We've got to kill those two," Ellis said heavily when they were half a mile away. "We'll never get to Trail City if we don't."

"Maybe," Trent said. "But today wasn't the time to try. They'd have killed us both."

"I reckon I knew that. But it galls me to take such a drubbing without putting up a scrap. We'll have to fight them somewhere between here and Trail City."

"Maybe — but we'll try to pick the time and place."

"I'll bet Fanok is the one who has registered the OT trail brand," Ellis said to Trent later. "The Sparks wouldn't want to take that brand when they already have the S Bar. Fanok and Cole seem to be close buddies."

Trent had no argument with that, but he had first claim to the brand and he wasn't bothered by Spark's announcement that they had taken the brand, too.

He moved the herd out, realizing that he had lost almost half a day to the S Bar herd. It was going to be hard to make up. He drove late and was just bedding down when he saw a rider coming into the camp area, stopping by the wagons.

Just as he reached the camp, Trent saw Al Rose leave the chuckwagon and dash toward the wagon where the visitor was talking to Beth Gilman.

Only when Rose threw himself on the little man did Trent recognize him. It was Vane Fanok, and Al Rose was doing his best to choke the life out of him.

Trent hurried forward. If Rose killed Fanok, that would be all Ira and Cole Spark needed to bring their big crew up here and start a battle that could have only one end.

CHAPTER 9

Before Trent reached the fighters, Beth had grabbed Rose and was trying to pull him off the little gunman. But Rose had a death grip on Fanok's throat.

"Get him off!" Beth screamed.

Trent grabbed Rose by the back of the neck and pulled hard. "Let him go, Al. You'll kill him. If you kill him, we'd have the whole S Bar crew up here after us."

"At least Fanok would be dead," Rose growled.

Fanok, still gasping like a fish out of water, got to his feet. "You'll hear about this," he choked.

"Consider yourself lucky," Trent said. "If I hadn't pulled him off, you wouldn't have any worries now."

"I'm sorry this happened, Vane," Beth said.

"It's not your fault," Fanok said, still breathing hard. "I should have smelled that skunk coming. He won't catch me napping again."

"I'd be satisfied if I never saw you

102

again," Rose said.

Fanok caught his horse and mounted up. Trent watched him, but suddenly his attention was caught by the way Al Rose was looking at Fanok. It was as though he were seeing a ghost.

"I'll deal with you later, Rose," Fanok said, glaring. "Before we get to Trail City, this whole drive will be swallowed up by the S Bar. But you're going to be my meat." He wheeled his horse and spurred him away in a gallop.

"Still think he isn't a spy?" Trent asked Beth.

"Why should he be spying?" Beth said. "They know that we're trying to get to Trail City as fast as we can. But wouldn't we like to know when they intend to try that swallowing act?" Beth frowned at Al Rose. "If I could have kept Vane coming here, I might have found out their plans, like I found out where they were hiding those supplies."

Trent nodded and turned away. He saw that Rose was staring after Fanok, and that puzzled look was still on his face.

"What did you see in Fanok just now, Al?" he asked.

Rose rubbed his chin. "I'm not sure. When he got mad, there was something about his face that seemed familiar. I feel like I've seen

Fanok before coming to Texas, but I can't put my finger on the place."

"Keep thinking," Trent said. "Maybe you'll remember. But you'd better get supper going now — you've got some hungry men to feed."

Trent got the herd on the trail early the next morning. He drove the herd harder than he liked to. He couldn't give the cattle time to graze enough to keep up their weight. But it would be better, he told the others, to get thin cattle to market than not to get any there at all.

Nearly a week after the OT stampede, he found that he could see the S Bar cattle behind him. The Sparks were driving their herd faster than Trent was. When night forced the men to bed down the cattle, he called them together, while Rose got supper by the chuck wagon.

"We've got to do something or the S Bar is going to overtake us and make good on that threat to swallow us up. Anybody got any ideas?"

"We could sneak down there tonight and start shooting," Andy said.

"You know what that would get us," Ott said. "Shallow graves."

There was silence for a minute, then Trent

took charge again. "I've got an idea if nobody else has. At least it might be worth a try — nothing slows up a drive like a good stampede."

Ott grinned. "If the S Bar herd stampeded halfway across Texas, it would keep them behind us for a while, all right."

"I figure it would take them a day, maybe two, to gather up their strays after a stampede," Trent said.

"Reckon we can make something happen to stampede that herd," Ellis said.

"We'll run them all the way back to the home ranch," Andy said enthusiastically.

While they were eating supper, Trent explained his plan. "Aaron, Andy, and I will take the first guard. About midnight, Bill, Dade, and Al will come out. Rose will watch the cattle. The rest of us will go down to the S Bar herd. We'll shoot in the air and wave our slickers. Then we'll get out of there quick."

"They'll know who did it," Tovar said.

"Knowing it and proving it are two different things," Trent said.

"I doubt if Ira Spark would care about proof," Rose grumbled.

"Anybody got a better idea?" Trent asked testily.

Trent got his supper and went out with

Andy and Ott to ride guard. He was tense as he rode slowly around the cattle. The wind was still blowing, but the OT cattle were quiet.

Shortly before midnight, three more riders came down from the wagons. Trent gave Rose his instructions, deciding at the last minute to leave Andy with him. If the S Bar herd ran, even going the other way, the noise might make these cattle restless. Rose wouldn't be able to hold them alone if they did. If the OT herd stampeded, too, they might go in the same direction as the S Bar, and the result would be what Ira Spark wanted. Besides, Trent didn't want the hotheaded Andy on this job. Andy howled when he got his orders, but he didn't change Trent's mind.

The S Bar herd was bedded down in a wide valley less than three miles behind the OT. Trent saw the herd was sleeping peacefully when they came over the rise that cut the valley off from the trail ahead.

Trent started to rein up to give out last-minute instructions when six horsemen suddenly charged them from the valley, a half mile this side of the sleeping herd.

"They're on to us," Ott said in surprise. "How could they be?"

"I don't know," Ellis said. "But look at

them come. We'd better get out of here or get ready to fight."

"Ride for it," Trent said, and wheeled his horse.

Back at the herd, Trent sent Andy, Ott, and Rose to bed. Tovar started slowly around the herd, but before Ellis began his circle in the opposite direction, Trent called him back.

"They were watching for us, Bill," he said. "That means somebody told them we were planning to come. Who?"

"I've been thinking about that. Nobody knew we had any idea of stampeding that herd except the men in our crew."

"It doesn't make sense that one of our own men would want the S Bar to overrun us," Trent said. "Who would be the traitor?"

"We know it isn't you or me," Ellis said. "And I'd trust Aaron Ott from here to Canada. That leaves Tovar, Andy, and Rose. The way Rose hates the Sparks, I can't believe it's him."

"That's cutting it pretty thin," Trent said. "Andy and Dade Tovar. Andy is a hothead, but I can't picture him making any deal with Ira Spark."

Ellis nodded. "That's cutting it even thinner. But how can we prove it?"

"I've been thinking that Ira Spark will

probably want a report on what we did after finding out they were expecting us. Wouldn't it be easy to make that report while you were supposed to be riding night guard?"

Ellis nodded. "I reckon. When the cattle are quiet, there's not much to do. I might not miss Tovar if he rode out for an hour."

"I'll stay on guard, too," Trent said. "If Tovar leaves, I'll follow him."

Trent moved around until he could see Tovar where he had halted his horse and lit a cigarette. Trent stopped, keeping his distance. Finally, Tovar moved his horse slowly on down the opposite side of the herd. Then, when he reached a gully, he cut sharply into it.

Trent nudged his horse into a slow walk around the herd toward the gully. When he got there, Tovar was gone. Trent didn't try to follow the course Tovar had taken. He angled for the trail leading back to the S Bar herd. He soon caught sight of a rider up ahead of him.

Trent followed the rider from a distance, sometimes losing sight of him. But he had no fear of losing him.

At the rim of the valley, he dismounted, ground-reined his horse, and walked ahead. The late moon was spreading some light over the valley, but nothing was distinct.

Trent saw Tovar riding toward the herd, and presently a rider came out to meet him. They talked for a few minutes, then Tovar turned and started back toward the top of the rise.

Trent hurried back to his horse and mounted, heading toward the OT herd. About a mile before he got there, he pulled off into a ravine and waited. When Tovar came even with the ravine, Trent stepped out, his hand on his gun.

"Where have you been, Dade?"

Tovar's hand dropped to his hip but stopped there as he saw that Trent already had a grip on his gun.

"What difference does it make?" Tovar grunted.

"You're supposed to be riding night guard. Ellis is alone there now."

"He'll make out," Tovar said.

Suddenly, Tovar dived at him from his saddle. Trent was caught by surprise. His gun was knocked out of its holster as he fell backward. He tried to catch himself, but Tovar's weight bore him to the ground. Tovar was several inches shorter than Trent, but he was also several pounds heavier, and he was using that weight to advantage.

"I don't have to tell you nothing," he grunted.

Trent rolled, throwing Tovar off balance. Before he could recover, Trent slammed a fist into his face. Heaving himself upward, he managed to unload Tovar. Both men scrambled to their feet.

Trent let Tovar come to him, lashing out at Tovar whenever he got close enough. He could outreach Tovar several inches, and he used that advantage to keep out of Tovar's reach while he landed stinging blows to his face.

With an oath, Tovar made a desperate attempt to close with Trent. But Trent landed a hard blow on Tovar's jaw, then side-stepped. As Tovar was wheeling to come again, Trent moved in and slammed two hard fists to Tovar's head, which rocked him to his knees. As he tried to get up, Trent hit him again. This time, Tovar only groaned and didn't try to get to his feet.

"Had enough, Dade? Ready to talk?"

"Nothing to talk about."

"I figure there is. Why did you go down to the S Bar herd?"

Tovar sat up and scowled, wiping blood off the corner of his mouth. "I went down there to see a friend. I knew you wouldn't allow it, so I sneaked out."

"You told your friend earlier last night

about our plans to stampede the S Bar herd, right?"

"No," Tovar grunted. "I just went down to visit, nothing else. I ain't fool enough to help the S Bar steal my own cattle!"

"Get back on your job, Dade," he said finally.

Trent didn't believe Tovar, but he knew he wasn't going to make him admit anything. He said nothing about Tovar to anybody but Bill Ellis. If others knew, it would stir up more trouble. And he had all the trouble with the crew that he could handle.

Two nights later, they reached the south bank of the Canadian River. Trent expected no trouble in crossing the river the next day, for it wasn't big here like it was down in the Territory where he had crossed it on other drives.

But his confidence faltered when he saw dark storm clouds rolling up in the west. When supper was over, he gave his orders for the night.

"Everybody will ride herd until the threat of storm is past," he said.

"We'll hold them," Ott said grimly.

Trent stationed the men around the herd, even assigning Rose a spot. Beth insisted on helping, so Trent gave her a place, too. She hadn't been bragging when she said she could make a good hand — she was a better hand at driving and holding cattle than her brother.

Trent took another turn around the herd to see if everything was all right. Suddenly he stopped. He was at a gap in the circle of riders that Al Rose was supposed to be guarding. But Rose wasn't there. He had disappeared.

CHAPTER 10

Trent urged his horse along, looking for Rose. He met Ellis just beyond Rose's post.

"Seen Al?" Trent asked.

Ellis shook his head. "I've had my mind on that storm," he said. "Coming from the northwest, like it is, if the cattle should spook and run, they're almost sure to go southeast."

"I know," Trent said. "They'd head right for the S Bar herd."

"How long before we get to Trail City?"

"About two weeks," Trent said, "if we don't have Spark trouble."

"We'll hold them," Ellis said. "I'll move up a little to cover part of Rose's area in case he doesn't get back."

Trent nodded and reined around. Andy, on the other side of Rose's post, would have to cover more area, too. Trent couldn't understand why he had quit his post during the storm.

Andy hadn't seen Rose, either, but he agreed to watch a longer stretch along the rim of the herd. Trent rode on, keeping an eye on the herd. The lightning was closer, and thunder was rolling ominously over the hills to the west and north.

Then the rain struck. With the rain came the wind, sweeping the deluge down on the herd and the guards in blinding sheets. Lightning crackled and thunder boomed over the prairie. But the cattle didn't run.

Trent continued riding around the herd. They were all on their feet, their tails to the storm, their heads down. Some of them were bawling mournfully, but there was no sign that they would stampede.

For half an hour the rain poured down, then the wind died away and the rain fell steadily straight down. Even the slickers failed to turn all the water, and Trent's shirt was almost as wet as if he hadn't been wearing a slicker.

The lightning had slacked off, though the thunder still rumbled in a steady roll. But it was over and Trent sent Beth and two of the men back to the wagons.

After they had ridden off, Al Rose showed up. His horse was tired and muddy, and Rose was as wet as if he'd been swimming in the river.

"Where have you been?" Trent demanded.

"I made a little visit back to our friends

behind us," Rose said, and his face spread into a grin.

"Did you try to start a stampede?"

"Try?" Rose exploded. "That was the granddaddy of all stampedes. The lightning and thunder had them ready to run. All I had to do was wave my yellow slicker a little."

"It's a wonder the Sparks didn't shoot you," Trent said.

Rose laughed. "They were too busy. Most of the S Bar riders were at the lower end of the herd trying to keep the cattle from drifting with the storm. I was up at this end."

"Better hit the sack now," Trent said. "We'll all need a good hot breakfast in the morning."

The rain didn't let up until almost dawn. As the hours dragged on and the rain continued to fall, Trent began to worry about the river crossing. Last night it would have been a simple matter, but after a night of hard rain the situation might be different.

As soon as it was light, Trent rode down to the bank of the stream. The Canadian was high; not out of its banks, but the water was swift and dirty. And the approach to the water, which had been fairly dry last night, was now a sea of mud and water holes.

By the time the sun was out, shining on

the water-soaked land, Trent and most of the crew were at the riverbank, examining the depth of the mud.

"If we drive them in at full speed, they might get through," Ott said. "Once they hit the water, they'll be all right. It isn't too swift to swim."

Trent agreed. "The water is no problem. But how about the north bank? That side is probably as boggy as this one. I'll ride over and see."

Trent's horse struggled to get through the mud on the south side of the creek. It seemed to suck him down like quicksand. Once in deep water, the horse swam strongly to the far bank. There the mud was just as springy and grasping as it was on the south bank. The horse struggled, but made the solid ground.

"We can't make it, can we?" Ellis said despondently when Trent got back.

"It's a mighty soft bog," Trent said.

Ott bit his lip and studied the hoofprints in the mud. "It will be a mighty tough crossing, but I vote to try it."

Trent looked at the others. All were here except Andy. He had gone out with the herd, which was grazing to the south. One by one, the men nodded.

"Then we'll try it," Trent said. "We'll take

just a few head the first time and hit the bank on the run. If they make it, we'll try the rest."

Trent left Beth and Andy to hold most of the herd. With the other men, he cut out twenty head.

"Once you start them," Trent warned, "keep them moving. If they stop in that mud, they'll have to be dragged out. Bill, you and Dade ride point. Aaron and I will pop them over the rump."

He gave the signal, and the men whipped the little bunch of cattle into a wild run.

"Keep them headed for that spot we marked!" Trent shouted at the men on point.

The lead cattle hit the mud. They floundered and tried to turn back, but Tovar and Ellis cut their backs with the rope whips and forced them to plunge ahead. The first ones broke through to the swift water and then the others strained to reach it.

They got all twenty into the swift water, but the worst was still to come. The cattle would have no head start to help them when they hit the boggy mud on the north bank.

The first of the cattle reached the bank. They struggled out into the mud, lunging with mighty heaves that seemed to get them nowhere. Tovar and Ellis kept slapping them.

Finally, the one out in front, a powerful

steer, lurched out of the mud, falling down when his feet hit solid ground. But he scrambled to his feet and lumbered away from the river.

Then the others struggled out. When the four riders got to the bank, they had nineteen cattle across the river. One, a cow that was too weak to make it, was bogged down belly deep in the mud.

"We'll have to pull her out," Trent said.

He flipped his rope over her horns and turned his horse. Ellis rode out to the cow, grabbed her mud-covered tail, and slapped the brush end of it against the saddle horn where he could hold it better.

The cow groaned as the two horses hauled it toward the bank. As soon as the cow was out of the hole, she began to struggle again and Ellis let go of her slimy tail. Trent pulled her toward the bank. When they got the cow to the bank, she was bawling furiously.

"Watch the old rip when you take that rope off," Ellis warned.

"I don't intend to play games with her," Trent said.

When he got the rope off the cow's horns, she made a lunge at Trent's horse, but Ott and Ellis moved in and drove her off.

They brought more of the herd across, fifty at a time. Each time some of them failed to make it through the mud and had to be dragged out with ropes. It was past noon when Rose called the crew to dinner.

As soon as dinner was over, Trent sent the men back to work. They left the weaker cows till last, hoping that the hot sun would dry up the mud a little. But Trent could see that the continuous stirring of the mud by hundreds of frantic hoofs was making the bog worse. The mud wouldn't dry until it was allowed to settle.

Downstream half a mile, Trent found another place where the mud had begun to dry. He decided to cross the remainder of the herd here. The mud was less troublesome, but even then, when the last drive had been made, there were twelve cows down in the mud.

"We'll be tailing those critters out till midnight," Tovar complained.

"It will be sunup if we don't hurry," Trent grunted, and again drove his weary horse into the mud.

Lanterns lighted the bog when the last cow was dragged out of the mire. The men were almost too tired to eat. Trent felt like a slave-driver when he assigned a man to ride guard. One could do it tonight. The cattle weren't frisky enough after that crossing to cause trouble, and it was impossible for the S Bar herd to get to them. There was a river between the herds that wasn't easy to cross; Trent could vouch for that.

But just before he fell asleep, he heard bawling to the south. The S Bar had completed the roundup of their scattered herd and was pushing the cattle up to the river to bed down in spite of the late hour. Tomorrow morning they'd be right behind the OT herd again.

With the first light of dawn, Trent had the OT riders moving. By sunup, the herd was being pushed out on the trail. Across the river he saw the S Bar herd beginning to move, too, and knew that his own determination to keep ahead of the S Bar herd was matched by the Sparks' determination to catch up and overrun the OT herd. There were almost two weeks of hard trail ahead. Trent wondered if his own determination and that of his men would be enough to match the drive of the S Bar men.

At noon, when Trent turned back to check on the S Bar, he found the bulk of the herd already across the river. The extra time had dried the muddy banks of the river considerably, for it didn't appear that the S Bar was having much trouble, although the herd was being brought across in sections rather than in one continuous drive. They'd be across and up the trail a few miles before dark. The OT had gained only a few miles by the stampede.

Two days later, it seemed to Trent that they had lost what little they had gained. He pushed the cattle hard that afternoon until he knew he had to stop to let them graze before bedding down for the night. Before supper was ready, he rode ahead to do some scouting. So far, they had had little trouble avoiding the few ranches in way. But he wanted to spot any obstacle that might be ahead so he could swing around it without losing time.

He had ridden over the first knoll from camp when he was surprised by a rider spurring up out of a gully on his left. His hand dropped to his gun but he stopped when he found himself staring into the bore of a rifle.

"Just leave the hardware alone," Cole Spark said, nudging his horse toward Trent. Another voice cut in from his right. He wheeled to see Ira Spark riding toward him from another gully. He had ridden into a trap.

"Laying for me?" Trent asked.

"Came up scouting," Cole said with the satisfaction of a man who had been given just what he wanted. "Saw you leave camp.

These gullies were handy so we used them. Didn't want you shooting off any guns and starting a stampede of your cattle."

"Very considerate of you," Trent said. "I'm not going to shoot any guns now, so put up yours."

Cole shook his head. "Not just yet. Get off your horse and shuck your gun belt."

Trent stepped down and slowly unbuckled his belt. When it fell to the ground, Cole and Ira dismounted, leaving their rifles. But Ira held his .45 on Trent while Cole moved up close.

"If we fired a gun here," Cole explained patiently, "every OT man would be here in two minutes. But there are other ways of killing a man." He held up a hamlike fist. "Not as noisy but just as effective."

Trent shot a look at Ira. Ira was taking off his gun belt.

"We were getting along all right till you butted in, Trent," Ira said. "With you dead, I figure we'll get along all right again."

122

CHAPTER 11

Trent watched Cole intently. He didn't think that Ira would start the swinging. Age was against Ira, and Trent expected him to stay on the fringes of the fight, getting in a lick now and then. He'd guarantee that Cole didn't lose this fight.

But Ira threw the first punch. It caught Trent on the side of the head and rocked him back on his heels. Cole leaped in before Trent could regain his balance and slammed a fist into his face.

Trent felt the blood spurt from his nose as he was pushed back. He stumbled and fell, seeing Cole leaping for him as he went down. Trent rolled the instant he hit the ground and Cole missed. He got to his feet just in time to meet a charge by Ira. He saw now that Ira wasn't going to stay on the sidelines.

Trent was still a little foggy from the two quick blows he had taken, but his mind was clear enough to know that he had to keep out of their grip. He was no weakling but both Sparks outweighed Trent by forty pounds — and none of that weight was flab.

Trent met Ira's charge with a stinging fist to the face, then he ducked away before Ira's reaching arms could clutch him. He was tempted to stand and slug it out with Ira. But if he tried to stand toe-to-toe with one of them, the other one would jump him and he'd be dead.

As Trent ducked away from Ira, he saw Cole charging at him like a bull. He dodged, landing only a glancing blow as Cole swept past. But before he could turn to face Ira, he was hammered on the neck and shoulder. He back-pedaled quickly, trying to get both men in front of him.

Cole charged him next, and he stood his ground long enough to stop him with a straight fist to the chin. Cole grunted and backed off, although he didn't go down. Trent watched him stagger back, knowing that he could knock Cole out now if he could follow up his advantage. But Ira's fist slammed against his ear, and he wheeled to face the older man. He caught another fist in his midriff.

In spite of himself, he doubled over, trying to catch his breath. Then Ira bore in, bringing up a fist that sent him sprawling. Trent jerked his elbows under him the moment he hit the ground, ready to roll away if Ira dived at him. As he moved, his arm hit a rock that gouged into the flesh. Ira was hesitating, looking at Cole.

Trent reached behind him and found the rock. It was about twice the size of his fist, rough on one side, affording him a good grip.

He glanced at Cole, who was still standing as though dazed, shaking his head. He heard Ira grunt, and he rolled quickly to one side without looking. He felt the weight of the big man hit his leg but he managed to pull free and roll to his knees.

Trent swung the rock, bringing it down hard against the side of Ira's head. The big rancher collapsed like a steer that had been dropped with a sledge hammer.

Trent scrambled to his feet as Cole came out of his daze and charged again, but he was so wobbly that his knees almost refused to hold him. He could see that Cole was little better.

He met Cole's charge head-on. It was like the clash of two battle-weary range bulls. Neither had the strength to knock the other over. But even the weakened charge was almost more than either of them could take. Cole slapped a fist against Trent's head that he could normally have shaken off like a fly. But now it sent him reeling. Cole tried to follow up his advantage and Trent braced himself, slamming a fist into Cole's face.

Cole went down, staggering several steps backward before he fell. Trent shot a glance at Ira, but he was still stretched out. He rushed at Cole, who was just getting to his feet again, slammed a fist into Cole's face, then threw his entire weight against his chest. Cole staggered backward again and fell heavily. Trent paid no attention to Ira, but lunged on top of Cole.

Cole continued to fight, but his blows were too weak to drive Trent back. Trent slammed his fists repeatedly into Cole's face until the big man dropped his fists and begged Trent to stop.

"All right," Trent panted. "But I'll kill you unless you tell me where the money is you and Fanok stole from me."

"What money?"

Trent slammed a fist into the side of Cole's face. "The money you stole in Trail City."

"Don't hit me again," Cole whined, cringing as far from Trent as he could.

"Then talk," Trent panted. "If you don't, I'll beat you till you're dead."

"All right," Cole wheezed, "I'll tell you."

Cole's eyes stared wildly at Trent, his breath coming in short bursts.

Trent drew back his fist. "I won't wait, Cole."

"There was a girl with us," Cole said hoarsely.

"I know that," Trent said, recalling the girl's voice he had heard that night just before he passed out. "Who was she?"

"Dance-hall girl," Cole said.

"Did you give her the money?" Trent demanded.

Cole nodded. "She took it so you wouldn't get it if you caught up with us."

"So it's in Trail City, yet. Where does she work?"

"In Sparrow's," Cole said.

"What's her name?"

But before Cole could say another word, a rifle spanged and the bullet dug into the dirt a few feet behind Trent. Trent wheeled, losing his seat astride Cole. Ira Spark was ten feet away with a rock in his hand. But right now, he was standing as still as a statue, one foot ahead of the other, in the position he'd been in when the rifle spoke.

Trent wheeled his glance to the top of the knoll. Zola Tovar was up there, sitting on her horse, the rifle still at her shoulder. Trent remembered that she often saddled her horse after camp was made and took a short ride. She said she got tired of bouncing along on the wagon all day and wanted to get out and feel the wind in her face.

127

Trent ran toward his gun belt. He was aware that the Sparks were both running, too, and he expected to feel the weight of one or both of them slam into him at any instant. If he could only reach his gun, there would be no more hand-to-hand combat today.

Trent got his gun clear of the holster and wheeled toward the Sparks. They were both in the saddle and were spurring their horses down the valley, keeping the ridge between them and the OT bedding grounds.

Trent brought up his gun and lined it on the back of Cole Spark, but he couldn't pull the trigger. It was one thing shooting a man when he was facing you with a gun in his hand — it was something else to shoot at a man's back.

He lowered his gun and picked up the belt, quickly strapping it around his waist as Zola came down the slope toward him. He ran to his horse and caught the reins. If he couldn't shoot the Sparks in the back, he could give chase and bring them to bay. When they started shooting at him, he'd have no compunction about shooting back.

"Wait!" Zola called.

"I can't wait and catch those two," Trent said.

"Let them go. You'd have to chase them

a long way to catch them. By then, they'd be close to the S Bar crew, and you wouldn't have a chance."

Trent realized Zola was right. The Sparks did have a good lead, and he probably wouldn't catch them until they were close to the S Bar herd.

"What was the fight about?" Zola asked.

"They made up their minds to beat me to death," Trent said. "Figured they'd have no trouble with the rest of the OT crew if they got rid of me."

"That's probably right," Zola said, dismounting. "You've been the fire that made men out of those boys. But when I came over the hill, it looked to me like you were doing the beating. Were you trying to kill Cole?" She smiled and moved closer to him.

Trent's guard came up. He recalled the last time Zola had played up to him; it had caused trouble between him and Andy.

"I'm glad you did waste at least one shot," he said, wishing he was on his horse now, instead of standing so near Zola. He turned his head so that he could see the top of the knoll. He wasn't surprised when he saw Andy coming down the slope toward them, drawn by the sound of Zola's rifle shot.

Trent stepped back to his horse. "Andy's coming," he said. "Must have figured there was a fight over here."

"He's a little late," Zola said, but she turned back to her horse, too.

Andy came down the slope, spurring his horse hard. "What's the shooting about?" he demanded, sliding his horse to a halt.

"I only heard one shot," Trent said, and he knew that Andy's rage wasn't directed at any unseen danger.

"The Sparks were set on beating Jason to death," Zola explained. "I took a hand and they ran. Must have thought all our men were right behind me."

She swung into the saddle and, lifting the reins, galloped up the slope toward camp.

After she had disappeared over the knoll, Andy swung down in front of Trent. "I thought I told you to let Zola alone," he snapped.

Trent scowled at Andy. "I'm not bothering her. And it's none of your business if I am."

"She's my girl," Andy said. "She told me so herself."

"All right. If she's your girl, what are you worrying about?" Trent turned away disgustedly.

But Andy wasn't through. He grabbed Trent's arm and spun him around.

That was too much for Trent. He'd just

been in a fight for his life with the Sparks and now Andy was insisting on pressing an argument that didn't interest him at all.

Andy had a fist drawn back as if to hit Trent, and Trent responded almost involuntarily. His fist lashed out and caught Andy on the jaw. Andy staggered back, lost his balance, and sprawled on the ground. Trent stepped over and stared down at him, but Andy made no effort to get up.

"Now look, Andy," Trent said hotly, "it's none of your business what Zola and I do. She doesn't interest me, if that's any consolation to you. But if you say one more word to me about her, I'll beat the pants off you. Is that clear?"

Andy nodded, but he made no attempt to get up. Trent wheeled and stepped into his saddle. He looked back once when he was halfway up the hill. Andy was just getting on his horse.

When supper was over, Rose called Trent over to the chuck wagon where he was washing dishes.

"I just remembered where I saw Vane Fanok before," he said. "Thought you might like to know."

Trent nodded. "I sure would. He helped rob me of all the money I owned and a lot that I borrowed."

"I don't know if what I've got to tell will be any help to you. You know, I ran a store in Dodge City for a while. Fanok was a gambler there. I saw him at the Long Branch more than once. He bought some things in my store a time or two, but he didn't try to cheat me."

"Is that all you remember about him?" Trent pressed.

Rose rubbed his chin. "He was in some kind of scrape in town, but I can't recollect what it was. Maybe it was with some girl there."

"Girl?" Trent asked, his interest quickening as he thought of what Cole Spark had told him about leaving the money they'd stolen from him with a girl. "Do you know her name?"

Rose sighed. "Can't even be sure there was a girl, but it runs in my mind there was."

Trent knew that Trail City, up the Arkansas River from Dodge City, was made up mostly of those who had moved there from Dodge to get rich off the trail herds. That fit into the pattern, all right, although it wasn't much of a clue.

The only sign Trent saw of the S Bar the next few days was the pall of dust that hung over the back trail.

Then one morning six riders intercepted

the herd. Trent, riding on the flank of the herd, spurred his horse forward.

"What's up?" he asked.

"You the boss of this drive?" one man asked.

Trent nodded. "What can I do for you?"

The man waved his hand at the other five riders. "We're from the ranches you've passed the last forty miles. I'm Abe Bartlett. We figure you might have picked up some of our stray cattle. We want to cut your herd."

Trent nodded. "Reckon that's fair enough. I think we do have some strays. What brands do you represent?"

Bartlett rattled off five different brands. Trent knew that they did have two or three cows in the herd carrying one of those brands.

"Our road brand is OT on the right shoulder," he said. "We'll help you cut the herd. See that dust behind? That's another herd and we want to keep out of its way."

Bartlett nodded. "Don't blame you. We won't hold you up long. We'll want to cut that other herd, too. We'll hold them up longer than you. They've got a bigger herd."

Trent nodded, getting some satisfaction from that. But what if Ira Spark refused to let the trail-cutters go through the S Bar herd? There weren't enough trail-cutters to force the issue. If Spark kept the S Bar herd moving, the time the OT herd lost here might give the S Bar the advantage it needed to overtake the smaller herd.

Trent called the men together and they swung the herd into a circle. All hands helped and the strays were quickly cut out. However, before they had finished, the S Bar herd came in sight.

"That's good enough for us," Bartlett said. "We don't want to hold you any longer. Move your herd on and we'll wait right here for the next one — know who's ramrodding it?"

"Ira and Cole Spark," Trent said. "That's the S Bar. We lost some cattle in a stampede one night. They got into that herd and Spark wouldn't let us cut them out. Mind if a couple of my boys stay with you and cut our OT cattle out?"

"No. In fact, I'd be glad to have a couple more men. We don't intend to let that herd go by without cutting it."

Trent kept Bill Ellis with him and sent the rest of the men ahead with the herd, telling Ott to push them hard.

Before the S Bar herd reached the spot where the trail-cutters were waiting, Trent saw Ira and Cole Spark break away from the herd and gallop forward. They would scream when they saw Trent and Ellis with the other men. And they might fill the air with more than screams before the dust cleared.

CHAPTER 12

Ira and Cole Spark slid their horses to a halt in front of the men, blocking the trail.

"What in blazes are you doing here?" Ira shouted.

"We're repping for some ranchers along the trail," Bartlett said calmly. "We figure on cutting your herd for any of our cattle that you may have picked up along the trail."

"We haven't picked up any cattle!" Cole Spark shouted. "Now, get out of our way!"

Ira pointed a finger at Trent. "What's that scum doing with you?"

"We just finished cutting his herd. He says some of his cattle are in your herd, and we figured we'd help him cut them out while we're getting our own."

"He's not cutting our herd!" Ira Spark shouted.

"Now, we figure different," Bartlett said, shifting slightly in the saddle so his gun was pushed forward within easy reach. The men behind him did the same.

Ira Spark looked back at the slowly moving herd. He made a motion, and half a dozen riders broke away from the herd and came forward. Trent wondered if Ira Spark would risk a gun fight over this. Obviously the trail-cutters were prepared for such an eventuality. Ira Spark turned back and glanced at the trail-cutters, who returned the glare without flinching.

"How long do you think it will take you to cut the herd?" Ira asked finally.

"A while," Bartlett said, his muscles relaxing. "You've got a big herd. But we'll do it as fast as we can."

"All right," Ira said finally. "We'll hold them for an hour, no longer. If you're not done then, you won't finish. And Trent doesn't go near the herd."

"He goes with us," Bartlett said. "The more men we've got working, the quicker we get the job done."

"No OT cattle are leaving this herd," Ira Spark shouted. "They're mine."

Bartlett looked at Trent, then back at Spark. "Never heard of one man bossing two herds."

"They're mine!" Ira screamed. "Trent won't get them."

"I don't believe in mixed herds," Bartlett said tightly. "We'll help cut out the OT cattle and send them up with the OT herd."

Trent thought Ira Spark was going to fight.

But he gradually subsided and reined his horse to one side while Trent and Ellis and the other trail-cutters began work.

Trent was in no hurry. Every minute spent here gave Ott that much more time to get the OT herd farther away. He soon discovered more strays in this herd than there had been in his. Trent had given orders to his men to turn away any strays that were attracted to his herd as they moved past the ranches. It was clear the Sparks had given no such order.

Trent found the OT cattle quickly. They were bunched fairly close together along one flank of the herd. He and Ellis had cut out twenty of the twenty-one Spark had said were in the S Bar herd by the time the cutting was half done.

"Let's take what we've got and get out of here," Ellis said nervously. "We're going to have trouble enough as it is catching up with our herd before Spark sends some gunmen after us."

"I reckon," Trent agreed.

He rode over to the leader of the trail-cutters and explained the situation.

"Hit the trail with them," Bartlett said. "These Sparks are a tough bunch, it strikes me. They must have done a little encouraging to pick up this many strays. We'll stall them here till you're well on your way."

Four of the trail-cutters were holding the cattle cut out of the S Bar herd. The OT cattle were being held separately. Trent and Ellis pushed the OT cattle away from the others and headed north, driving them hard.

It was late afternoon when they caught up with the rest of the herd. Trent had expected Cole or Ira Spark to lead a half-dozen men after them. But Ira Spark either had some other strategy or else the trail-cutters had held them so long they hadn't had time to catch up with Trent and Ellis.

Trent had the herd moving shortly after sunup the next morning. As soon as the herd was strung out, he rode back to get a bearing on the S Bar herd. He was disappointed when he discovered the S Bar only a few miles behind.

They crossed out of the Territory and into Colorado. Trent saw the bleached buffalo bones that Martin Culver had used to mark the boundaries of the trail. After wandering across the Texas panhandle and the Territory, it was almost like getting home to see those skulls and know that he was on the right trail.

Trent drove until sundown. He put three men on guard, dividing the night between the six riders. Rose said he should ride night guard in Beth's place, but she would have none of that.

"You're the cook," she said. "You have to roll out early and get breakfast. All I have to do is eat it. I'll take my share of night guard."

Trent took his turn at guard on the same shift with Beth. He admitted to himself that he was guarding Beth as much as the herd. He'd never forgive himself if the S Bar struck while Beth was on guard and she got hurt.

Each morning, when Trent rode back to check on the S Bar herd, he found it a little closer than it had been the day before. But they were near Trail City before any attempt was made to stop the OT herd. It was Beth's sharp eyes that alerted Trent. Trent had assigned Beth to the first watch.

The cattle were still feeding when Beth reported that she had caught a glimpse of some horsemen off to the west, riding north. Trent called Bill Ellis and Andy, and rode north and west to investigate. They found the riders sooner than they anticipated, stopped behind a knoll.

The riders were surprised by the three OT men and opened up with six-guns. Trent reined up sharply. They were still out of effective range of a handgun, and it was so dark now that only luck could direct a bullet accurately.

"Let's get out of here!" Andy shouted.

"Hold it!" Trent snapped. "They aren't going to hit us with those guns. Let's use our rifles."

He jerked his rifle out of its boot and opened fire. The five riders wheeled their horses and rode southwest.

Nothing else happened to slow their progress, and two days later they reached the Arkansas River in midafternoon. Trent and Aaron Ott rode ahead to scout for a crossing. Ever since hitting Colorado, Trent had seen signs of heavy traffic ahead of them. He had thought, coming north as early as they were, that they would be ahead of most of the herds coming out of Texas. Now he realized that they were not the first — others had come up the trail of the skulls, and they had been moving fast.

But he wasn't prepared for what he saw when he came over the rim of the valley of the Arkansas and saw the herds on the north bank of the river.

"Would you look at that!" Aaron Ott exclaimed. "Must be ten thousand cattle up there."

"We may have trouble selling our herd," Trent admitted. "But at least we got here without being run over."

"Where are we going to graze our herd in that mess?"

"Not on this side of the river, that's sure," Trent said. "There are only a couple of herds over here now. But if we stop here, Spark will camp right beside us. We're going over on the other side — maybe even beyond town."

They found the river calm. There had been no rain the past week, and Trent saw that it was going to be easy to cross the herd.

They selected a spot to make the crossing and rode back to meet the herd. Trent passed the word to the others, and there wasn't any hesitation when they approached the river. The wagons rolled across the river, and the herd followed. The last of the cattle reached the north bank of the Arkansas at sundown.

"We'll push on north of town, bed down, and tomorrow we'll see about a buyer," Trent said.

He led out, swinging the herd to the west to go around the swampy land that flanked Cheyenne Creek, which ran into the Arkansas south of town. After crossing the little stream and moving up into the choppy sandhills northwest of town, Trent found a little valley where the grass was still good.

"We'll bed down here," he told Ellis, "and we'll post a heavy guard."

"Not much Spark can do now with all these other herds here," Ellis said.

"I won't rest till we sell the cattle. Spark will stop you and Ott from selling if he can."

Ellis nodded. "I reckon you're right."

The night passed slowly for Trent. To the south there was a continuous bawling from restless steers. Others answered the complaints and the night was filled with their laments.

After breakfast the next morning, Trent and Ellis rode to town.

Trail City was bustling with activity. Trent found it hard to believe this was the same town he had passed through less than two months ago. The main street, called Trail Street — it was directly in line with the trail from the south if a man drove his herd straight on without veering — was churned into a bed of ankle-deep dust and sand. Both the Longhorn and Sparrow's were busy.

They pushed their horses up to the crowded hitchrack and dismounted. Trent asked about buyers, and the bartender jerked a thumb toward a man surrounded by drovers. Trent pushed his way into the circle and waited his turn. The buyer seemed interested when he said he had cattle to sell.

"Fine," the man said. "How many? What road brand?"

"We've got about two hundred and fifty to sell," Trent told him. "The rest of our herd is going on to Nebraska. Road brand is OT."

The man's head snapped up and he stared at Trent; then he shook his head. "I'm afraid I've got about all I can handle. There are already too many cattle here for the market."

Trent was tempted to grab the man and demand an explanation, but then he spotted Ira Spark at the far end of the bar, and suddenly he understood.

"Wonder if Spark has reached all the buyers," Trent said softly to Ellis.

"Only way we'll find out is to talk to the rest."

Trent pushed his way to the bar. "How long has he been here?" he asked the bartender, nodding toward Spark.

The bartender looked at Spark. "He came in late last night. Spent the night here and was waiting for the first man to show up this morning. He must have a lot of cattle to sell."

Trent turned to Ellis. "That answers our question."

On the porch of the hotel, Trent stopped, touched Ellis's arm, and pointed up the street at the Longhorn Saloon. Cole Spark and Vane Fanok were just going inside.

"You look for the buyer, Bill," Trent said. "I want to keep an eye on those two. They might be looking up the girl who has my money."

"Sure," Ellis said, and went inside the hotel.

Trent moved across the street and up to the swinging doors of the Longhorn. His only chance to recover his money, he was sure, was to find out who the girl was who was keeping it for Spark and Fanok and take it from her before they got it.

Cole Spark and Vane Fanok were at the bar drinking, but there wasn't a girl in the saloon.

The two came out soon and wandered down to Sparrow's place. Trent followed, dropping into a chair inside the door. With so many men milling around the room, he had little fear of being seen. But they made no contact with any of the girls. In fact, they didn't even show any interest in the girls who were moving around, coaxing the men to buy them drinks.

Trent was discouraged when they turned toward the door. He ducked low in his chair, and they passed him without a glance. He got up and followed them outside.

Cole and Fanok turned south toward Print Olive's Trail's End Stable. They had probably left their horses there. One thing Trent felt sure of — they wouldn't be going there to meet the girl with the money.

Trent waited in front of Sparrow's. If Cole and Fanok rode out of town, he'd find Ellis and see how he was faring in his search for a buyer for their cattle.

But suddenly the murmur of the town was split by gunshots. A man tottered out of the stable and staggered up the street toward the saloon.

It was Al Rose. Trent hit the street running. He was only vaguely aware of the two riders coming out of the stable and heading their horses south toward the creek.

He was the first to reach Rose. There was blood on his shirt front in two places, high on his chest and low, almost in the abdomen.

Trent caught his arm and helped him to the side of a building, where he sank down.

"Who shot you? Spark? Fanok?"

Rose nodded, tried to speak, but was barely able to get the words out. "Fanok. That girl . . ."

"What about her? Who is she?"

Rose tried again, but his voice was even weaker. "That girl . . . is . . ."

That was all. Trent felt Rose slump to one side, and he knew he would never find out what Rose had learned about the girl he wanted to find.

CHAPTER 13

Trent stood up, facing a half-dozen men who had gathered.

"Will somebody get the undertaker?"

One man nodded and turned away. Ellis came running down the street from the hotel and stopped beside Trent.

"Somebody said it was an OT man," Ellis panted. "I thought it might be you. Who shot him?"

"Fanok," Trent said.

"Starting to whittle us down?"

"I think this had something to do with Dodge City when Rose ran a store there."

The undertaker came and Trent made the necessary arrangements. Then he and Ellis got their horses and started back toward camp.

"Find a buyer?" Trent asked.

"None that Spark hadn't already seen," Ellis said grimly. "He really put the fear in them. They wouldn't take our cattle if we gave them away." He twisted in the saddle and looked back at the town.

"There must be some buyer there who has a little backbone."

"Not enough to buy our cattle," Ellis said. "There are ten or fifteen thousand head of cattle around town and probably twice that many coming up the trail right now. Why should a buyer risk being black-listed or killed to buy two hundred and fifty head of cattle that aren't even in very good shape?"

"You've got a good argument," Trent said. "Probably the same argument Ira Spark is using."

The OT camp was solemn that night. Plans were made for Trent to go to town with the Tovars and the Gilmans to Al Rose's funeral the next morning. Ott and Ellis would stay with the cattle. There was little danger of trouble. The S Bar herd was being held on the south side of the river, and there were too many other herds between them for the Sparks to do anything drastic.

"After the funeral, what?" Beth asked. "Andy and I have some steers we want to sell. We can take them on to the place we're going to settle and sell them later, and Dade and Zola could do the same. But what about Aaron's and Bill's cattle?"

Trent shook his head. "I've been beating my head on that question all day. If we could

149

hold our cattle here till the S Bar sells and the Sparks go home, the buyers would probably take ours."

"Ira or Cole would stay here to make sure they didn't," Ellis put in.

"I'm afraid you're right," Trent agreed. "If we can't find a buyer tomorrow, I suggest we head north for Ogallala. We wouldn't have to contend with the Sparks there, and the Gilmans say they're going to settle in the sandhills beyond Ogallala, anyway; maybe the Tovars, too. This would be right on their way."

"That sounds great," Andy said enthusiastically. "We can let them graze more and pick up the fat we've run off them."

Trent's plan was approved by everyone so it was decided to lay over tomorrow, attend Rose's funeral, and look for a buyer. There was little talk of selling in Trail City now. Everyone had resigned himself to the fact that no buyer here was likely to touch the OT stuff. If they couldn't sell, they would point the herd north up the Colorado-Kansas border, then angle across the southwestern corner of Nebraska to Ogallala.

Trent put Andy on first guard, not anticipating any trouble. But before anybody had gone to bed, visitors came.

"I want to see Bill Ellis and Aaron Ott,"

Ira Spark called.

"What about?" Trent asked.

"I've got a proposition to make."

"Ride on into the light."

Cole Spark was with his father. Ellis and Ott moved forward, and Trent went with them.

"What's on your mind?" Trent asked.

"Nothing so far as you're concerned," Spark said sharply. "What I've got to say is for Ellis and Ott."

"We're listening," Ellis said.

Ira started with a question. "First, I want to know something. Are Tovar and the Gilmans moving out of Texas permanently?"

"That's right," Ott said. "But what's that got to do with Bill and me?"

"I want you to move out with them. You can keep the cattle you have if you'll get your families and the rest of your stuff out of Texas."

"We can't even sell the cattle we've got here," Ott said.

"I can arrange that," Ira said. "But you've got to get out of Texas and stay out."

"We figure on staying," Ellis said.

"You won't stay there on my land!" Ira Spark shouted. "I'm giving you a chance to get out with a whole hide. If you don't take

151

it, I won't be responsible for what happens to you."

"You leave us alone and we'll get along all right."

"Nobody stays on my land unless he works for me!" Ira shouted.

Trent found it hard not to take a hand. He didn't understand how any man could be so pigheaded and greedy. Ira Spark sounded as if he actually believed what he said. According to Ellis, Ira Spark not only didn't own the land that Aaron Ott and Bill Ellis lived on, he didn't own much of the other land he claimed for the S Bar.

"Show us your deed to the land we live on and we'll move," Ott snapped.

"I'll show you six feet of ground to be buried in!" Ira screamed. "That's all the land in Texas you'll ever own."

"You're not running us out," Ellis said flatly.

"You'll never sell your beef!" Ira screamed. "I'll see to that. And you'll never get back to Texas, either!" He wheeled his horse and jabbed him with the spurs. The horse leaped into a dead run, and Cole spun his horse and followed.

When they turned back to camp, Trent saw Dade Tovar watching Ellis and Ott with something like fear in his face.

"You sold us all out," Tovar said finally to Ellis.

"We didn't sell out anybody," Ellis retorted.

"How do you figure they sold you out?" Trent asked, moving up where he could see Tovar better.

"If they'd taken Ira up on his proposition, he wouldn't have bothered the rest of us any more. Now he'll see to it none of us sell one hoof."

"If he stops us here, we'll go on to Ogallala," Beth said. "I'm glad they didn't knuckle under."

Tovar subsided like a sulky boy, but Trent knew he wasn't convinced that there wasn't big trouble ahead. Remembering that Tovar had been slipping out to visit someone in the S Bar camp, Trent wondered how much Tovar knew about Ira Spark's plans.

He changed his mind about leaving only one man on guard and put out two. He had never seen a man more furious and unreasonable than Ira Spark had been when he left here tonight. He might do anything.

But nothing happened, and when morning came, the men discussed the possibility of trouble during the day and agreed that it was practically nonexistent.

"Aaron and I will stay here while you go

to the funeral," Ellis said. "If you find a buyer in town, send him out. We're ready to make almost any kind of deal."

"I'll start looking for a buyer as soon as the funeral is over," Trent said. "Ott can come in to town and help after the women get back here."

Trent paid his quarter and ate dinner at the hotel dining table with over a dozen cattle-buyers and drovers. The funeral had been short and simple, with only the OT hands there.

He spotted a buyer that he and Ellis hadn't talked to yesterday, and as soon as the meal was finished, he accosted the man. But this buyer's reaction was the same. He'd gotten the word from Ira Spark not to deal with the OT.

Trent checked at the Longhorn and Sparrow's before going down to the loading pens. When he had passed through Trail City early this spring, these pens were being built. Now they had the look of heavy wear and tear. Here and there boards were broken and nails were loose. But the pens were serving their purpose.

He turned back toward town, his decision made. There was no point in wasting any more time. Trail City would not buy the OT herd as long as Ira Spark was around.

Trent went past the Trail's End Stable and headed for Sparrow's Emporium. Before he got to the Emporium, however, he saw Bill Ellis riding in from the north end of town. He waited for him.

"Dead as last year's grass up there at camp," Ellis reported. "Beth said she wanted something to do, so she went out to watch the cattle and keep them from grazing too far away and told me I might as well come on in."

"Nothing doing here, either," Trent said.

Ellis sighed. "I was afraid of that, but I got impatient waiting." He swung down and tied his horse in front of Sparrow's. "What do we do now?"

"Pick up the men and get ready to pull out for Ogallala in the morning," Trent said. "I was just going into Sparrow's, figuring some of the men would probably be here."

Together they pushed through the swinging doors. Trent saw all three of the OT men playing cards with three other men. He wondered how much Andy knew about playing cards. He was probably losing what little money he had.

Trent touched Ellis's arm and stopped him as he started toward the table.

"Things are getting pretty hot there," he said softly.

Ott had noticed something that wasn't according to rules. He was staring sharply at the man directly across the table from him.

"Keep your hand above the table, Mister, when you're shuffling the cards," Ott said.

"Think I'm cheating?" the other man snapped back.

Ellis nudged Trent. "I know that jasper," he whispered. "Aaron ought to know him, too — he's an S Bar man."

"Fast with a gun?"

"The fastest," Ellis said.

Trent started toward Ott, but Ott's eyes were riveted on the man, his face flushed with fury.

"I know you're cheating!" he yelled. "You've slipped cards into that deck the last two times you've handled them."

"Let it go, Aaron!" Trent snapped.

But Ott was too angry to notice. Trent glanced at the men across the table from the OT riders. All were on the alert. Ott wouldn't be fighting one man, but all three of them.

"It's a trap, Aaron!" Ellis said.

The S Bar gunman flipped a glance at Trent and Ellis. "This is his fight, not yours. Stay out of it. Nobody says I cheat and lives to brag about it."

Trent looked at all those around the table.

Andy was staying with Ott, but Tovar was already inching his chair back to get out of the way. It would be Ott and Andy against the three men. As Ellis had said, it was a trap. The cheating probably had been deliberate, so obvious that Ott couldn't miss it.

Suddenly the S Bar man lunged backward, drawing his gun with a sweep of his hand. Ott and Andy threw themselves backward, too, both digging for their guns. But Ott didn't move fast enough to get out of the path of the gunman's bullet.

The S Bar gunman ignored Andy and wheeled on Trent. Trent was aware that Dade Tovar had kicked his chair backward and was cringing against the wall. The two men with the S Bar gun fighter were pulling at their guns.

Trent's first shot spun the gunman around and he fell heavily. Ellis's shot caught one of the other men and spun him around, too. The one S Bar man still on his feet dropped his gun and raised his hands.

Before the startled spectators in the saloon realized that the fight was finished, the remaining S Bar man had picked up the man Ellis had wounded and was taking him outside. Trent stepped over to look at the gunman who had started it all — he wouldn't be starting any more fights.

Trent turned to his own crew. Tovar was still cringing against the wall. Andy was getting up, apparently unhurt. But Ott wasn't getting up.

CHAPTER 14

Trent dropped to one knee to examine Ott, who was twisting and groaning.

"It's my arm," Ott said.

"Looks like it's busted," Ellis said, kneeling beside Trent.

"Go find a doc, Andy," Trent said, and Andy ran outside as though glad to get away.

The doctor set the arm and put on splints. Before he was through, the undertaker who had taken care of Al Rose came in and took the S Bar gunman's body away. A man wearing a badge came in and asked some questions. Trent expected a show of authority, at least, but after a few questions, the lawman shrugged and walked out again. His arm in a sling, Ott got up and went out of the saloon with Trent and Ellis.

They found Dade Tovar at camp. He had nothing to say about backing off from the fight, and Trent didn't mention it.

"Reckon that was a trap to put me out of action," Ott admitted while they were eating supper that night. "They'll try something on you next, Bill."

"I'm not going to be sucker enough to get into a card game with Spark's best gunslick," Ellis said.

"He wasn't in the game when it started," Ott said. "We were winning, too, till he started cheating."

"Was the cheating obvious?" Trent asked.

"Sure. A two-year-old could have slipped cards into the deck slicker than he did. I was too mad to think about it being a trap. Anyway, he didn't kill me — thanks to somebody else's shooting."

"You won't be able to ride, though," Andy said.

"I will be soon," Ott said. "I'm not going to let a busted wing keep me out of the saddle."

"You'll have to ride in the chuck wagon for a few days," Trent said.

"Who's going to drive it now that Rose is dead?" Andy asked.

Trent looked at Beth. "How about you, Beth?"

"Doesn't look like I have much choice," Beth said. "Maybe Aaron will soon be able to drive it."

"Maybe," Trent said. "Sometimes, though, it takes two good hands to drive a team. Aaron will have only one."

Trent readied everything for the trail before he went to bed. It was going to be a relief to get on the trail. The stop here in Trail City had cost the OT crew one dead and one wounded, both at the hands of the S Bar. They couldn't afford any more casualties.

At dawn the next morning, after an early breakfast, Trent gave the order to move the cattle off the bedding ground. He saw one advantage to this reshuffling of jobs. Beth was a better cook than Al Rose had been. But he was going to miss Beth and Ott with the herd. There were just four riders to keep the herd moving now. Trent and Ellis agreed that they would take turns riding point and drag. Andy and Tovar would ride the flanks.

Trent had checked the course carefully as he came down, for he had planned to take a herd of his own up this trail to his ranch in the Nebraska sandhills. This was the only really long strip between here and Ogallala that he felt might have to be made without water. The little draws and creeks might have water in them, but he couldn't take the chance. He wanted these cattle to get plenty of water and grass between here and Ogallala and put back some of the fat they had lost on the drive up from Texas.

"We'll swing to the west," Trent told Ellis as they started the herd moving. "There isn't much water straight ahead until we hit the south fork of the Smoky Hill. But there is a good-sized lake a few miles to the west. We'll water there."

While they were eating dinner, letting the cattle graze, Trent noticed a small cloud in the south. He recognized it for what it was — dust. Apparently some other herd waiting at Trail City to find a buyer had given up and was heading for Ogallala, too.

He rode drag after dinner and, once the cattle were moving well, he turned back and kicked his horse into a lope. He couldn't leave the herd long but he had to identify the herd behind him.

The only possible reason for the S Bar to make such a drive would be to satisfy Ira Spark's burning fury. If he could swallow up that herd, he might consider it worth the extra effort.

When Trent came in sight of the herd, he reined down into a ravine. The ravine ran into a valley that paralleled the course of the herd, and he rode boldly down the valley until he was sure he was almost even with the herd. Then he rode cautiously to the top of the hill separating the valley from the cattle. There was no mistaking the proud bearing of one of the men riding point — Ira Spark.

Trent turned his horse back into the valley and headed him north again. The race he thought had ended at Trail City was turning into the home stretch. And the OT crew was handicapped. Instead of six riders, Trent had only four, including himself, to push the herd. The S Bar had lost a man killed and another wounded, but in a crew of fifteen or twenty, two wouldn't be missed.

Trent caught up with the herd again by midafternoon. He found the drags scattered some, but he soon crowded them into the herd. Then he rode up one side of the herd till he overtook Andy.

"Move them along faster," he told Andy. "Pass the word to Dade and Bill. I'll crowd the drags a little."

"What's the rush?" Andy asked.

"There's a herd behind us."

They drove later than Trent had originally intended but were fortunate in finding water in a little stream. Now they could turn straight north and forget about swinging west to find water. They'd hit the south fork of the Smoky Hill River before too long.

"Tell us it's Spark behind us and have it done with," Ellis said when they met at the chuck wagon.

Trent nodded. "It's the S Bar, all right. We've got another race on our hands."

"Only this time Ira is more determined than ever," Ellis said.

"We're going to have to stop and fight him somewhere," Ott said from the back of the chuck wagon. "I'll be able to get in the saddle tomorrow."

"Not that soon," Trent said. "And we can't stop and fight the S Bar. We might try to lose them by turning off the trail, but we can't go west to Denver — not enough water. We can't go east into Kansas because of the quarantine. If we try to beat them to Ogallala, it's going to mean a mighty hard drive."

"If Aaron can drive the chuck wagon," Mrs. Gilman said, "I can help him do the cooking. Then Beth can get back with the herd."

"Reckon I'll need everybody I can get," Trent admitted. "But you've got your own wagon and chores to tend to."

"I'll manage," Mrs. Gilman said. "If I don't do everything I can to beat Ira Spark, I'll feel like I'm letting Reuben down."

Trent turned to the others. "How do you feel? Want to make a run for Ogallala?"

Tovar shrugged. "We have no choice."

Ellis and Ott nodded. Trent turned to

Beth, and she eagerly added her approval.

Relieved of her cooking duties, Beth took her turn at night guard. Trent was finding it harder all the time to keep his mind off her. He wished she didn't have to make a hand on this drive. Not only was it work that a girl shouldn't have to do, but there was added danger in it. If the S Bar should make another attempt to stampede or steal the herd, they might try it while Beth was on duty. She'd be gunned down like a man. But as long as she was in the working crew, there wasn't much Trent could do.

Ott drove the chuck wagon the next day, although Trent knew it caused him plenty of pain. The herd covered a lot of miles before Trent called a halt for the night, but the dust cloud remained behind them.

As the days struggled past, the herd walked north on weary legs. Sore feet made cattle lag and pushing along the drag became a bigger and bigger job. They crossed the south fork, then the north fork of the Smoky Hill River, stopping only long enough to water and rest briefly.

It was shortly after they had crossed the south fork of the Republican that Trent, riding point, saw Bill Ellis spurring his horse toward him. He reined up.

"What's wrong?" he demanded when Ellis

got close. "I thought you were pushing the drags along."

"I was," Ellis shouted, and Trent could see the rage twisting his face. "Three S Bar riders surprised me and stole them — over twenty head."

Trent frowned. "It's a wonder they didn't shoot you, too."

Ellis nodded, his anger subsiding a little. "Reckon so. But we've got to go back and get the cattle."

"We can't do that," Trent said. "We'd be walking right into a trap."

When they hit the Arikaree fork of the Republican, it was night and Trent called a halt. He was sure that the S Bar hadn't gained on them today. If the S Bar kept the OT drags they had taken from Ellis, that might even slow them down. Those cattle couldn't keep up with the pace. That was the reason Ellis had been so far behind the main herd today when the S Bar men overtook him. But Trent was guessing that Spark was letting any sore-footed cattle he had drop behind and leaving a couple of men to bring them along at their leisure. Otherwise, the S Bar herd couldn't maintain the pace it was.

"How much farther before we cut northeast toward Ogallala?" Ott asked as he finished his coffee.

"We'll turn down this creek," Trent said.

"Won't that take us into Kansas?" Ellis objected.

"Just a few miles of the northwestern tip of Kansas," Trent said. "I don't think anybody will enforce that quarantine law here. This creek runs into the north fork of the Republican just over in the edge of Nebraska. When we hit that junction, we'll head north toward Ogallala."

"How long before we get there?" Beth asked.

"Should make it in a week if nothing happens," Trent said.

Trent gave the cattle little time to graze the next morning before he headed them northeast down the Arikaree. He hoped the S Bar would miss their turn and go on north. But before noon, he had confirmed the fact that the S Bar had turned down the Arikaree, too.

"They're gaining on us," Ellis reported shortly after noon.

Trent nodded. "I know. They must be leaving their drags for a couple of men to bring along later. Only their fastest cattle are in their lead herd."

"Can we keep ahead of them?"

"We're going to try."

They reached the confluence of the Arikaree and the north fork of the Republican and crossed, heading northeast. When they hit a small stream that Trent had heard called Buffalo Creek, he called a halt. The grass was good here, and he resolved to let them graze a little later the next morning. If they got too weak, they couldn't keep ahead of the S Bar. And no buyer would touch them when they got to market.

"Fill all the barrels with water," Trent said as they finished breakfast the next morning. "The next water is on the Frenchman, and we won't hit it till tomorrow."

Dust was already rising behind them when Trent lined the herd out to the north. He drove late and had to get the herd moving early the next morning to keep ahead of the S Bar.

They reached the Frenchman late in the afternoon. As they rode through the sandhills south of the creek, Trent had twice seen the vanguard of the S Bar herd. It was closer now than it had been at any time since they left Trail City.

"How far to Ogallala from here?" Ellis asked worriedly.

"About fifty miles," Trent said. "I'd like to take four days, but we'll probably have to do it in two or get run over."

They pushed the cattle up on the flat land

a couple of miles, where they fell to eating. Trent decided to let them fill up; they'd start early in the morning.

When Trent rode in for supper, he noticed that one man was missing.

"Where's Bill?" he asked Ott.

Ott looked up in surprise. "I don't know. I hadn't missed him."

Trent's lips were pressed together in a tight line as he turned to look back at Frenchman Creek where the S Bar herd was just coming into sight.

CHAPTER 15

"You don't suppose he went back to the S Bar camp, do you?" Ott asked.

"I don't know," Trent admitted. "He's been as edgy as a wounded bear ever since those riders took the drags away from him. He swore he'd get them back, but I don't believe he'd be crazy enough to try it alone."

"He knew you wouldn't help him," Ott said. "What are you going to do?"

"If he doesn't show up for supper, I'll go looking for him."

"I'll go with you," Andy volunteered quickly.

Trent shook his head. "I'd better go alone. If he has gone to the S Bar camp, the only chance I'll have of getting him out alive is to sneak him out. If anybody goes with me, it will just mean more noise and less chance of dragging Bill out of there."

Trent finished his supper and went to his saddled horse. It was almost dark. If Ellis had an idea of getting his cattle back, he'd surely wait for night. There was a full moon less than an hour high in the eastern sky.

170

Trent rode south slowly. That moon wasn't going to allow much sneaking around tonight. Ellis must be loco to think he could do any damage at the S Bar camp alone. But Bill Ellis hadn't been thinking straight since the S Bar took those cattle.

Daylight was gone, and only the bright moonlight shone on the prairie when Trent reached the creek. As he had expected, the S Bar had camped on the south side of the creek after watering the herd. Trent crossed the creek a half mile above the camp and rode slowly downstream.

Suddenly gunfire erupted ahead and to his right at the edge of the hills. Trent nudged his horse into a run toward the sound. After those first two shots there was a short silence. Then a fusillade of shots rang out.

The noise was too much for the cattle. They got to their feet and began lumbering downstream. It wasn't a stampede — the cattle were too footsore for that. But they were moving, and Trent saw riders break away from the firing along the foot of the sandhills to the south and head back to turn the cattle.

Trent spurred his horse. He knew he'd find Bill Ellis there and he'd be in deep trouble. The fact that the guns were still firing meant that Ellis was alive.

From the flashes of the guns, Trent guessed there were four or five men shooting at somebody in the wash. He swung to the right to hit the wash back between the hills, where the S Bar men wouldn't see him. He reached the wash and dropped down into it, then ran in a crouch toward the flash of Ellis's gun.

Before he got there, the men behind the sagebrush along the slope started running forward in short, zigzag advances. Trent counted five men, and he knew that Ellis would never be able to stop them, even if he was lucky enough to hit one or two.

It was long range for Trent's gun, but he stopped and began shooting. He wasn't sure that he hit anything, but the addition of his gun to the battle put a different outlook on the fight from the S Bar viewpoint.

They turned and scurried back up the slope, and they kept on going toward their horses. They must have decided that the rest of the OT crew was joining in the fight, Trent thought.

He was sure they'd go just far enough to get reinforcements. He ran forward, still crouching. When he got close to the spot where he had seen Ellis's gun flashing, he called his name.

"Here," Ellis said. "Sure glad to see you."

"What are you doing here?"

Ellis swore softly. "Acting the fool, I reckon," he said. "I thought I'd come over here and start a stampede and maybe steal twenty head of Spark's cattle to make up for the ones they stole from me."

"Fat chance you had of doing that alone," Trent said. "Why didn't you say something about it?"

"Reckon I knew you'd veto it," Ellis said.

Trent caught a groan that Ellis tried to pinch back. He leaned forward. "Are you hit?"

"In the leg," Ellis said.

"Let's have a look."

The moonlight wasn't strong and Trent couldn't tell how badly Ellis was hurt, but he knew he'd need help getting out of there. And they'd have to get out in a hurry.

Trent asked, "Where's your horse?"

"He's back on the other side of that hill," Ellis said, pointing. "I left him so I could sneak up here for a better look. I bumped into old Ira himself. I don't know what he was doing out here, but we didn't discuss the weather when we met — we just started shooting."

"Where is Ira?"

"Down the wash a ways. He won't be going anywhere."

173

"You killed him?"

"Reckon so. I should have done that years ago, back in Texas."

Trent lifted Ellis on his good leg. "We've got to get out of here fast. You've really stirred up a hornet's nest."

Ellis swore softly, partly from the pain. "I reckon I have. You should have knocked me in the head before I rode down here."

"I would have if I'd known you were coming," Trent said.

Trent kept looking back over his shoulder as he helped Ellis out of the wash and over the ridge.

"Think you can ride all right?" Trent said when they found Ellis's horse.

"Don't have much choice," Ellis said. "I'll make it. Where's your horse?"

"Not far away. You start for camp. I'll catch up with you."

When they reached the OT camp, Trent found those not on guard waiting expectantly.

"We heard the shooting," Ott said. "What happened?"

"Bill killed Ira Spark. Then four or five S Bar men cornered him in a wash. They were fixing to even the score when I took a hand. Guess they thought our whole outfit was there, for they turned tail and ran. Bill got hit in the leg. Can you fix it?"

"I'll get some hot water," Mrs. Gilman said. "There's a little left over from the dishes."

"What will they do now?" Andy asked worriedly.

"Just what you think they'll do," Trent said. "Fill your canteen and ride out and take the guard. Send in Beth and Tovar."

"Going to leave me out there alone?" Andy asked, starting to fill his canteen.

"Not for long," Trent said. "We're moving out. I want to talk to Beth and Tovar first."

Andy didn't argue. Trent helped dress Ellis's wound and get him in the wagon. By then, Beth and Tovar had ridden in from the herd.

"What happened down there?" Beth asked anxiously.

Trent quickly explained. "I figure Cole will come over here red hot to kill every one of us to avenge Ira."

"Let's get rolling," Ott said. "I can ride now, so I'll take Bill's place. I'll help Andy start the herd north. The rest of you can hitch up these wagons."

In thirty minutes, the OT outfit was moving north under a bright moon. Trent pointed the herd a trifle to the east of the North Star.

175

The night passed peacefully. The next day Trent kept the cattle moving until the sun was halfway up in the sky. When the heat began to bear down, he called a halt.

"We'll let the cattle graze, and we'll get what rest we can," he announced. "Then we'll move out again late this afternoon."

"Nobody's chasing us," Andy complained wearily. "Can't we wait till tomorrow to go on?"

Trent shook his head. "See that little cloud of dust rising back there? The S Bar must be moving out."

"How did they get those cattle together so soon?" Tovar said.

"I doubt if they ran far," Trent said. "Those cattle are just as tired as ours. The S Bar crew probably didn't get any sleep last night, either — they had a funeral to take care of, you know."

At four in the afternoon, Trent roused those who were sleeping and got the teams hitched up. Before five the herd was moving again. The S Bar herd was stirring up dust, but they were still six or eight miles back.

The cattle were bawling thirstily as they started north. They had had no water for a day, and they would get none until they hit the South Platte. With time, Trent might have swung the herd northeast from the

Frenchman to water at a little creek called the Stinking Water. But there was no time. He planned to make the next stop the South Platte.

Dawn was just beginning to pale the light of the moon when Trent caught the change in the tone of the bawling. The cattle in the lead suddenly threw up their heads and picked up the pace. Before long the entire herd was moving forward almost at a trot.

Then Trent caught it himself. The early morning breeze was coming in from the north and there was a smell of water in it. As the dawn light got stronger, Trent could see the flat plain breaking away ahead of them. Dimly he caught sight of the hills on the far side of the river. Between those hills and where they were now was the South Platte River, and on the north side of the river was Ogallala.

The men driving the wagons gained new spirit as the pace of cattle and teams increased. They hit the first of the draws that ran into little canyons and reached down to the river, a mile or more away.

"Let them go!" Trent yelled. "But keep them spread out when they hit the river."

He galloped on ahead of the cattle, cutting back into the draw. When the cattle reached him, he split the herd, making the thirsty cattle spread out so that they wouldn't all try to drink at one place.

While the cattle were drinking, Trent helped unhitch the teams and lead them down to water. It was well after sunup when the work was done.

"It's not going to be easy to cross, for a fact," Trent said, surveying the river. "But the water seems to be low. We shouldn't have any real trouble."

As it was, he got the last of the herd across the river by noon. He guided the cattle out into the hills north of the town and held them in a valley there.

"When are you going into town?" Ellis asked from his bed in the chuck wagon.

"I'm so tired I couldn't bargain with a buyer now," Trent said.

Ellis nodded. "I reckon that's right. I figure we're safe enough from the S Bar now. This is a civilized country. Did you see all the farms we passed the last couple of nights?"

Trent slept like a dead man that night. Andy had to punch him twice to wake him to take his turn riding guard. It wasn't just weariness; it was partly relaxation. As Ellis had said, they had won the race. But the work wasn't over. There was still the big job of finding a buyer who would take the cattle.

Trent rode into Ogallala early the next

morning. There was plenty of activity here but nothing like Trail City, and things were more orderly. This town wasn't built just for the boom of an enterprise that was already fading rapidly. Ogallala was a solid railroad town. There were plenty of loading pens and there were a lot of cattle in them now. But most of those cattle had come from the ranching country in the hills to the north.

But his satisfaction in finding a town where the buyers wouldn't be dominated by the Sparks was short-lived. As he rode down the street, he saw Cole Spark and Vane Fanok disappearing into the Cowboy's Rest.

Trent rode on down to the shipping pens. Of the men perched on the fence looking at the cattle, he picked out two who looked like buyers. A few minutes of talking to the men rewarded him with the promise from one buyer to ride out and look at the herd.

"The owners are with the herd," Trent explained. "One has a bad arm, the other was shot in the leg."

"Must have been a rough trip," the buyer said.

"It was," Trent said. "And the cattle show it. But they're good stock. With a little time on grass and grain, they'll make fine beef."

They started away from the pens, but Trent reined up when someone called his name. At the far side of the pens he saw Herb Hartline. He had hoped to postpone his meeting with Hartline until he had a chance to recover his stolen money or sell Ellis's cattle and collect his share of that sale.

"Ride on out to the camp," he told the buyer. "Head north and veer a little west. You can't miss it. There's a man here I've got to talk to."

With a feeling of impending disaster, Trent reined around toward Hartline.

CHAPTER 16

The cattle-buyer rode on to the north while Trent turned toward Herb Hartline, waiting by a corner of the loading pens. Hartline was a blue-eyed man of medium build, a man that Trent considered one of his best friends. But Trent knew that Hartline had a greedy streak in him — that he always looked for the profit.

"You're back sooner than you expected," Hartline said when Trent reined up. "Got the cattle for your ranch?"

"I ramrodded a drive up from Texas," Trent said. "I got robbed in Trail City on the way down so I couldn't buy anything."

The smile faded from Hartline's face. "That's too bad. That puts both of us in a spot. I just bought out Schuman and Taggart on my north and came down to sell some cattle to get a little money. I was hoping you'd be coming soon with the three thousand you borrowed from me. I promised those two fellows I'd pay them when you got back."

"My cousin will share what he gets for his

cattle with me," Trent said. "But that won't come to three thousand dollars. Maybe I can raise the rest some way."

"I hope so," Hartline said. "I have to pay off Taggart and Schuman, even if it means selling that little place of yours."

Trent reined around, pinching back the hot words that sprang to his tongue. He thought Herb had loaned him the money partly out of friendship. But now he wondered if his only reason hadn't been his certainty that Trent's venture would be a failure and he would be able to foreclose on the ranch. It joined Hartline's on the south. If he bought out Taggart and Schuman on his north, the addition of Trent's place would make his spread a big one. If he foreclosed on Trent's ranch, he wouldn't sell it — he'd bet on that!

Trent started toward camp, but as he rode past the Cowboy's Rest, shots rang out inside, and a man burst through the swinging doors. Trent wheeled his horse to the hitchrack and threw himself from the saddle as he recognized Dade Tovar.

Even before he got to him, Trent saw that Tovar was hard hit. A man peered out of the doors of the saloon but didn't come through. Then as Trent reached Tovar and took his arm, looking for a place where he could lie down, men came running from up and down the street.

"Take me to camp," Tovar said. "Alone."

Trent turned toward his horse. He didn't see Tovar's horse, and he knew there was no time to look for it. Tovar was holding a hand to his lower chest, and blood oozed between his fingers.

"Who did it?" he asked as he helped Tovar to the horse.

"Fanok," Tovar said, reaching with one hand for the saddle horn.

It was pure determination that kept Tovar going now, Trent knew. He boosted him into the saddle, where he wavered back and forth, but held on.

Trent was sure that Tovar knew he would never get to camp, but he clung tenaciously to the saddle horn. At the edge of town, Tovar called to Trent in a hoarse whisper.

"I can't make it any farther. Help me off. I've got to talk," Tovar said. "Don't want anybody else to hear."

"I'm listening," Trent said, squatting beside Tovar.

Trent knew Tovar didn't want to talk to him, particularly. It was just that Trent was the only one on hand. For a moment he was alone with Tovar. Then another horse galloped up and slid to a stop. Trent looked up as Andy ran over to the building.

"I was in the Crystal Palace," he explained. "I came as fast as I could. Anything I can do?"

"Just listen," Trent said. "He wants to talk."

Andy crouched beside Trent as Tovar rolled his eyes at him, wide and a little frightened.

"I won't make it to camp," Tovar said weakly. "I wanted to see Zola — she's my wife."

"Wife?" Andy exclaimed. "She's your sister."

"Wife," Tovar repeated. "She's Vane Fanok's sister. Fanok was a gambler in Dodge; Zola a dance-hall girl. I wanted to marry her then, but Fanok wouldn't let me. This spring in Trail City, Fanok and Cole Spark made a deal. Zola was part of it. They let us get married, but I had to pass her off as my sister. I was to get a thousand dollars for helping them."

"Did it have something to do with stealing the cattle and land of the little ranchers down by the S Bar?" Trent asked when Tovar paused.

Tovar nodded. "Cole lost a lot to Fanok in a card game. He cut Fanok in on the deal to pay him off. I was to go along with Ellis and the others and report every move to Cole or Fanok. Zola was to play up to the men and start trouble among them if she could — and how she could!" Anger crowded up in Tovar's face, pushing out the pain for a moment. "When you showed up, you became her main target."

"Then you did tip off Spark about the stampede we planned?" Trent said.

"Sure," Tovar said weakly. "I'd do anything to keep Zola. But I hate Fanok and Cole. Zola wanted me but she wanted money even more, and she threatened to leave me if I didn't toe the mark. A week ago I found out Zola was carrying three thousand dollars Fanok and Cole stole from you, and I asked for a cut. I figured I was earning it by giving Zola a perfect front. But Cole and Fanok decided they didn't need me any longer, so Fanok picked a quarrel with me, and I was fool enough to try to outdraw him."

Tovar sank against the building, and for a moment Trent thought he was dead. But then he saw the jerky rise and fall of his chest.

Trent thought of the time back there in the Texas panhandle when he had slammed a rock against Ira Spark's head and had whipped Cole. He had crowded Cole to the point where he had admitted that the girl who had been with them the night they robbed Trent had the money. Cole was almost ready to tell him the girl's name when Zola fired that rifle shot and broke up everything.

He glanced at Andy, who was squatting against the wall of the building, his face almost as pale as Tovar's. Learning that Zola was Tovar's wife had been a real blow to Andy.

He turned to Tovar again. The man was slumped lower against the wall, and Trent shook him gently.

"Dade. Dade, can you hear me? Where is Zola now?"

Tovar stared blankly at Trent for a moment; then the fire came back into his eyes.

"You've got to kill Fanok for me," he said, his voice low and thick. "You're the only one who can do it."

"Where's Zola?" Trent repeated.

"With Fanok," Tovar said. "They're skipping out."

"What about the deal with Cole?"

"They say they'll meet him back in Texas, but they won't. Cole won't ever see them again. Neither will I!"

A sob shook Tovar's body, a shudder ran over his whole frame. He slid sideways and his mouth sagged open. Trent laid him flat on the ground and looked up at Andy.

"Is he dead?" Andy asked in a whisper.

Trent nodded. It amazed him that Tovar had managed to live as long as he had. Sheer determination to make Fanok pay had driven him to stay alive long enough to tell his story.

But what good had it done? While he had been here with Tovar, listening to his story, Vane Fanok and Zola had very likely been putting a lot of distance between them and Ogallala. Trent might never see them again, either. And if he didn't, he'd never get his three thousand dollars back.

CHAPTER 17

"Find the undertaker, Andy," Trent said. "Tell him to come after Dade."

"What are you going to do?"

"I'm going to look for Fanok and Zola. They may have left town already. But if they haven't, I intend to get my money back."

Andy hurried away and Trent went to his horse and mounted. He looked down the street. He didn't see Zola's horse at any of the hitchracks, but she might have put him in the livery stable. For that matter, he didn't see any S Bar horses, either. Cole and Fanok had most likely put their horses in the barn to give them a good feed of grain.

He headed for the barn. It was the best place to start his search for Fanok and Zola. But as he approached the Cowboy's Rest again, Cole Spark came out on the porch, glaring at Trent.

"Trent, get off that horse and fight like a man," Cole shouted.

Trent reined up. He didn't want to bother with Cole now. Every minute he delayed gave Fanok and Zola more time to get out of the country. But he could see that there was no denying Cole Spark. Given a few minutes, he could probably talk Cole out of his fighting mood — or slap him out of it. But he couldn't ignore him.

Trent dismounted.

"You're drunk, Cole," he said, letting the reins of his horse drag.

"You've been wanting a showdown with me for a long time," Cole said. "This is your chance."

"Where's your sidekick, Fanok?" Trent demanded.

Cole's face darkened. "I don't know," he said. "I ain't sure that he ain't double-crossing me."

"Why don't you go after him then, instead of me?"

"You stole the cattle that was ours," Cole said. "You made those weak-kneed clodhoppers rear up and fight, and one of them killed Pa. Now you're going to take my land, too."

"It's not your land," Trent said. "Ellis and Ott are going back there."

"I'll kill them!" Cole said thickly. "But I'll kill you first. If I don't have that land, I won't get Zola."

Trent hid his surprise. Still, it made sense, now that he considered it. Zola was a girl to

189

turn any man's head, and she was one to move in the direction where the money was.

"Go back and sober up," Trent said, making a last effort to get past Cole. "I've got work to do."

"You're going to pay for what you've done to me!" Cole screamed.

His hand dropped down for his gun. Even half-drunk as he was, his draw was swift. But not as swift as Trent's. Trent's gun roared first, and Cole's bullet dug into the ground in front of him as he staggered forward.

For a moment everything was quiet on the street, then men were crowding around Cole. Trent waited only long enough for witnesses to establish the fact that Cole Spark had drawn first. Then he mounted and started on toward the livery stable.

But again he was stopped. This time, it was Andy coming down the alley into the street.

"What happened to you?" Trent demanded, seeing Andy's torn clothes and the bruises on his face. Blood trickled from one corner of his mouth.

"I saw Vane Fanok and Zola running down the alley from the Cowboy's Rest," Andy explained. "I headed them off, but while I was arguing with Fanok, Zola hit me from behind. Then Fanok nearly beat me to death."

"Where did they go?"

"I don't know. But I think they were heading for the livery stable."

"How long ago was that?"

"Just a couple of minutes."

Trent dismounted and tied his horse at the hitchrack. "Then they must still be there — I haven't seen any riders leave town. Let's go down and see."

They started slowly toward the stable, crowding the fronts of the buildings. Trent searched as much of the front of the barn as he could see and the building across the street from it. Fanok and Zola had had time to get over there if they were laying an ambush, guessing that Trent would come for them.

Suddenly Andy stopped and caught Trent's arm. "Hold it, Jason. Somebody's coming."

Trent stopped and looked behind. Beth was riding down the street toward them. Trent tried to motion her back without shouting, but she rode on and reined up in the street in front of them.

"Bill doesn't like the price that the buyer offered him for the cattle," she said. "He wants you to come out and talk it over with them."

"I'll do that," Trent said, "but we've got business right here now."

"Get out of here, Sis!" Andy exploded. "We're liable to get shot at any minute."

"Shot at!" Beth exclaimed. "Who's shooting at you?"

"Nobody yet," Andy said. "But Vane Fanok and Zola are down here somewhere. Zola is Fanok's sister. She's been double-crossing us all the way up from Texas. They've got Jason's three thousand dollars and are trying to get out of town."

Beth looked at Trent. "Where is Fanok now?"

"We figure he's in the livery stable, which means you're pretty close to trouble — you'd better get back."

"How about you?" Beth exclaimed. "I don't want you and Andy to get shot."

"I don't intend to let Fanok ride out of town with my money," Trent said. "And I don't want you getting shot, either."

"This is man's business," Andy added.

"You're my brother," Beth said sharply. "And Trent — you've got to come back."

"I intend to," Trent said.

Beth sat on her horse in the street, not moving, while Trent and Andy stepped back across the boardwalk toward the front of the building. But before they reached it, a shot

192

rang out from down the street. Andy wheeled toward the sound, and Trent thought at first that he was merely looking for the source of the shot. Then he saw the tear in the sleeve of his shirt and knew he'd been nicked by the bullet.

Beth turned her horse and spurred him out of range as Trent turned toward the barn, his gun in his hand. But the shot had come from the building across the street from the barn. Trent was concentrating on that building when a shot came from the front of the barn itself.

Trent wheeled to face the barn. "Keep that gun in the other building busy," Trent said to Andy. "I'll handle the barn."

It was an ambush, all right. But apparently the marksman in the building across from the barn had been afraid his quarry was going to get away when Trent and Andy left Beth at the hitchrack, and he had fired too soon. Now Trent had both guns pinpointed.

"Suppose there are more than two?" Andy said, crouching behind two horses at the hitchrack.

"I doubt it," Trent said. "I figure one is Zola, the other Fanok. I'm going to get closer."

Trent dodged toward the corner of the

building. Shots rang out from both the barn and the building across from it, but Trent reached the corner and ducked around it without getting hit.

Andy's gun was roaring, the bullets slamming into the building across from the barn. Suddenly, a scream ripped the air, and Zola leaped through the door, holding a hand over her upper arm.

"I'm shot!" she screamed.

"Get back to your gun!" Fanok yelled from the barn.

Trent turned to look at the barn. There was no sign of Fanok, but as Zola continued to stand in front of the building across from the barn and scream, Fanok stood up at the front window of the barn and yelled at her.

Trent leaped out into the street where he could get a better view of the window. As he moved, Fanok wheeled and fired at him. The shot missed and Trent aimed and fired quickly.

Fanok yelled and straightened up, then toppled forward, the upper half of his body hanging through the window.

It was over. Zola was still standing in the street holding her arm. But she wasn't screaming now. She was staring at her brother, draped over the barn window.

Trent and Andy ran toward Zola before she recovered from the shock of being hit and decided to resume the fight. Andy wouldn't shoot again, now that he knew who he was shooting at, and Trent wouldn't if he could help it.

Andy reached Zola first. "She must have dropped her gun," he said.

"Make sure she doesn't have another one," Trent said.

Zola shook her head numbly. "I don't have a gun." She looked accusingly at Andy. "You shot me," she said incredulously.

"I didn't know it was you," Andy said miserably.

"Where's the money Fanok and Cole stole from me?" Trent asked.

"I don't know anything about any money," Zola said.

Trent wondered how he could have thought Zola was pretty. Now that her smile was gone, her face was as hard as granite. Hate blazed from her eyes.

"Dade said you had it," Trent said patiently. "You've been keeping it for Cole and Fanok since last spring."

"Try and find it," Zola said.

"I'll do that very thing if you don't hand it over," Trent said. "I figure you've got it in a moneybelt."

"What if I have?" Zola said. "You can't get it."

"Want to bet on that? I'll undress you right here in the street if I have to."

"I'll get the money belt for you," said Beth, swinging down in front of Zola.

"I'll give it to him," Zola snapped. She started to jerk the tail of her shirt out, but winced when she moved her wounded arm.

Beth took her other arm and turned her toward the building behind them. "Come on. I'll help you. This is no dressing room."

Trent wondered if Zola would turn on Beth once they were out of sight. But they were in the building only a minute before Beth led Zola back out. Beth had a money belt in one hand.

She held the belt out to Trent. "Here's your money. Now what do we do with Zola?"

"As soon as I make sure my money is all here, I'm in favor of turning her loose on Ogallala," Trent said. "That might be a dirty trick on the town, though."

"She's not that bad," Andy said quickly.

Trent examined the contents of the money belt. Most of the money was here.

"Let's get back to camp and talk to that cattlebuyer," he said.

"Bill thinks you could make good money

taking the cattle up to your ranch and fattening them out yourself," Beth said.

"I know that, but . . ."

Suddenly Trent got the excitement of the last few minutes out of his mind and began thinking straight. He didn't have to find an immediate buyer for Ellis's cattle in order to get some money to pay Herb Hartline. He had the money now that he had borrowed from Hartline. He'd give it back to him.

He could take Ellis's and Ott's cattle up to his ranch and fatten them. He couldn't think of a way he could make money faster this summer and fall. Bill Ellis and Aaron Ott could go back to Texas.

He turned to Beth. "I know a good piece of land just south of mine that Andy can claim."

"Then we'll be close neighbors," Beth said.

"Not for long, I hope," Trent said, looking closely at her. "I've got the cattle I need to run on my grass. But it's going to be mighty lonesome at the home place. Know what I mean?"

She smiled. "I knew it before you did."

Wayne C. Lee was born to pioneering homesteaders near Lamar, Nebraska. His parents were old when he was born, and it was an unwritten law since the days of the frontier that it was expected that the youngest child would care for the parents in old age. Having grown up reading novels by Zane Grey and William MacLeod Raine, Lee wanted to write Western stories himself. His best teachers were his parents. They might not have been able to remember what happened last week by the time Lee had reached his majority, but they shared with him their very clear memories of the pioneer days. In fact, they talked so much about that period that it sometimes seemed to Lee he had lived through it himself. Lee wrote his first short story in 1945. It apapeared as "Death Waits at Paradise Pass" in *Lariat Story Magazine.* In the many Western novels that he has written since, violence has never been his primary focus, no matter what title a publisher might have given one of his stories, but rather the interrelationships between the characters and within their commmunities. These are the dominant characteristics in all of Lee's Western fiction and create the ambiance so memorable in such diverse narratives as THE GUN TAMER (1963), PETTICOAT WAGON TRAIN (1972), and ARIKAREE WAR CRY (1992). In the truest sense Wayne C. Lee's Western fiction is an outgrowth of his impulse to create imaginary social fabrics on the frontier, and his stories are intended primarily to entertain a reader at the same time as to articulate what it was about these pioneering men and women that makes them so unique and intriguing to later gernerations. His pacing, graceful style, natural sense of humor, and the genuine liking he feels toward the majority of his characters combined with a commitment to the reality and power of romance between men and women as a decisive factor in making it possible for them to have a better life together than they could ever hope to have apart are what most distinguish his Western stories.